Christmas Cozy

by

Kathi Daley

Chapter 1

Frosty the Snowman blared over the loudspeaker as I helped my best friend, Levi Denton, set up for the first annual Ashton Falls High School Christmas Tree Lot. Levi is a coach and physical education teacher at the high school, and as a teacher, he was required to perform a certain number of adjunct hours each year. Because he hadn't logged any hours in the past two years he'd been asked—ordered—by Principal Joe Lamé to manage the tree lot, which would be staffed by students who'd volunteered to cover the various shifts. It was the Friday afternoon before the big opening, and a handful of staff and students had shown up to help Levi. Although I'm neither a staff member nor a student, it's a best friend's responsibility to share the pain of whichever member of the best friend triad is currently in the most need. The third member of our little group, Ellie Davis, would be along shortly to help out as well. Personally, I didn't think working the lot would be all that bad. The music was festive, the smell of the fir trees inviting, and everyone—except Levi—seemed to have embraced the Christmas spirit and shown up wearing their very best mood.

"Where should I leave these ornaments?" Chelsea Manchester, Serenity High School's head cheerleader, asked me.

I peeked into the box the perfectly coiffed beauty queen was holding. It was full of ornaments sporting the school colors (black and gold) and school mascot (bulldog).

"They're cute," I commented.

"The alumni association asked the cheerleaders to sell them door-to-door in order to raise funds for new uniforms," Chelsea explained.

"Yikes," I sympathized.

"I know, right? Like any of us want to traipse around town peddling these things. The girls were all set to rebel until Coach Denton took pity on us and kindly agreed to sell them at the tree lot."

"That was nice of him."

"Yeah." Chelsea smiled. "He's the best."

It looked as if the head cheerleader had a bit of a crush on the football coach. Levi was careful not to send the wrong signals to the girls who tended to follow him around, but he was young and single and quite a babe, so I knew that maintaining a professional distance was often a struggle. I can still remember the huge crush I had on my science teacher when I was a sophomore. He was both handsome and smart, and I just knew he secretly wanted to go out with me as much as I fantasized about going out with him. Of course, I was sixteen and he was twenty-six, but I didn't let that small detail derail my daydream.

It was such a letdown when I found out he was happily married with a baby on the way. So much for schoolgirl crushes.

"Lizzie Breeland and I both plan to help Coach Denton with the tree sales once the lot gets up and running," Chelsea said, referring to her best friend and fellow cheerleader. "We even ordered elf outfits online. The skirts are pretty short, but we figure we can wear boots, and the cashmere sweater we chose for the top should be plenty warm."

"I'm sure Coach Denton will be grateful for any help the cheerleaders are able to provide."

One thing was certain: if the Ashton Falls cheerleading squad showed up in skimpy outfits we'd sell a larger number of trees to adolescent males than Christmas tree lots normally did.

"It's the least we could do after Coach offered to take these ornaments off our hands." Chelsea grinned, showing off her perfect smile. "Besides, I heard Jett Jarratt and the guys from the team are helping out as well."

"Yes, Jett and the guys are helping Coach Denton unload trees in the back of the lot." I looked at the box Chelsea was still holding. "As for the ornaments, I guess we can store them in the cabin for now. I'll show you where to put them."

The location chosen for the tree lot was a retail property owned by Tom Jarratt, the father of Levi's star football player, Jett. Originally, the lot was going to be housed in a warehouse down the road, but the roof of the old warehouse had caved in just two days before the first trees were due to be delivered. Tom had jumped in to offer an alternate property at the last minute.

Levi had wasted no time in moving everything over to the new location, which, in his opinion, was going to work out a lot better than the original venue anyway. The large lot was right on the highway and featured a small, one-bedroom cabin that previously had been an antiques shop. The shop had closed its doors at the end of the summer and a new tenant hadn't been found as of yet. Which was perfect, because it would allow Levi to use the cabin as a home away from home during the two and a half weeks the tree lot would be in business.

Chelsea glanced over my shoulder. "It looks like you have a visitor coming this way. I'll just set the box inside the door and then go to see if I can help the guys."

I was turning to see who the cheerleader was referring to when I was engulfed in a bear-size hug.

"If it isn't little Zoe Donovan." I struggled to breathe as high school teacher Holly Jolly— yes, that's her real name—wrapped her arms around me, forcing my face into her ample bosom. While I am admittedly petite Holly is a large woman with an equally large personality.

"It's nice to see you, Mrs. Jolly," I replied once I'd been released and was able to take a step back. "I see you brought your camera. Are you here to take photos?"

Mrs. Jolly had been my history teacher when I was a freshman, although I'd heard she'd switched to senior history this year.

"Please call me Holly," Mrs. Jolly corrected me. "And yes, I'm staff adviser for the school newspaper this year, so I thought I'd get a few shots. The lot looks fantastic. I especially love the fact that you hung colored lights on the cabin and then strung all those little white lights everywhere else. It gives it such a festive feel."

"The lights were Zak's idea." I referred to my fiancé, Zak Zimmerman, who was also an alumni of Ashton Falls High School.

"Zak always did have a creative streak," Mrs. Jolly commented. "I still remember the set decorations he designed for the holiday play when he was a freshman. I have to say they were truly inspired. Some of the best I've ever seen."

To be honest, I'd forgotten all about that.

"I hear congratulations are in order," Mrs. Jolly added.

"Yes, Zak and I are engaged," I confirmed.

"Your ring is simply lovely," Mrs. Jolly said. "Classic and elegant, yet simple. I always knew the two of you would end up together," Mrs. Jolly said with confidence.

"Really?" When I was a freshman in high school I considered Zak to be my archnemesis. Other than those times when Zak would give me stupid gifts like cartoon sweatshirts or join Levi, Ellie, and me for lunch just to annoy me, we really didn't hang out together all that often. Although looking back, I really did love those sweatshirts and my heart did pound just a tiny bit harder when Zak invaded the sanctity of our best friend lunch table.

"I noticed a spark from the very beginning." Mrs. Jolly beamed. "When I watched the way you each tried to gain one-upmanship on the other I knew you were destined to be together. The sparks you created when you clashed were truly electrifying."

"Electrifying?"

"Like tiny bolts of lightning," Mrs. Jolly confirmed. "So where is Zak today? I'd like to say hi while I'm here."

"He's picking up the sleigh he rented," I informed the woman. "He's going to play Santa and hand out candy canes to the kids who visit the lot. We were just going to set him up in a chair near the cash register, but he insisted that Santa needed to have a sleigh, and with all the snow it was easy to transport it through town."

"What a wonderful idea," Mrs. Jolly exclaimed. "I was afraid the venture would be an unorganized mess, but it looks like you and Levi have things well under control."

An unorganized mess?

"Levi wasn't thrilled with the assignment, but he's worked really hard to pull it all together before opening day tomorrow," I informed the portly woman, whose cheeks were generously dusted with bright red blush the same color as her sweater.

"I see many of the team members are here, helping with the setup," Mrs. Jolly commented as the background music changed to a jaunty rendition of "Rudolph the Red-Nosed Reindeer."

"Yeah, almost half of the guys from the football team showed up, and of course Boomer is here as well."

Boomer Jarratt was Levi's assistant coach.

"While I'm sure Levi appreciates the help, there are a couple of young men, including Jett Jarratt, who really should be home studying for this semester's final exams. If Jett doesn't get at least a B on my test he'll flunk senior history. I'm afraid if he doesn't get his act together he won't graduate in the spring."

"Wow. Really? That would be a shame. I heard Jett has an excellent chance of getting a football scholarship to some pretty good schools. In fact, Levi told me there are two or three that are actively pursuing him."

"I've heard that as well, which is why I've been on him to study harder and turn in his assignments on time. It really would be a shame if he didn't graduate, but you know kids these days. They don't understand the consequences of their actions. I've tried to work with him, and I even offered to find him a tutor, but he refuses to get the help he needs. Lou Barton told me he's flunking math as well. I'm afraid it really won't be looking good for the boy unless he buckles down and focuses on his schoolwork."

I knew Mr. Barton was a tough teacher but also a huge supporter of the athletic program, so I was willing to bet he'd pass Jett whether he actually passed the class or not. Mrs. Jolly, on the other hand, tended to grade by the book.

"Have you spoken to Levi about it?" I asked. "Maybe Jett will listen to him, even if he isn't listening to anyone else."

"Perhaps I should speak to Levi. I know he receives a copy of all of his athletes' midterm grades, but perhaps he doesn't understand how serious things have gotten. Thanks for the suggestion."

"Anything I can do to help."

Mrs. Jolly turned, as if she was going to leave. Then she stopped and looked around. "By the way, as long as I ran into you, I wanted to ask about Hometown Christmas. I know you're on the committee. I'd like to assign some of the students on the newspaper staff to cover the main events. I'd do it myself, but I'm tied up that weekend. I don't suppose you have a schedule I can work from?"

"I can e-mail it to you. The event has been reduced from four to three days this year. The Santa Village strolling carolers, street vendors, live nativity, and sleigh rides will be in place Friday, the nineteenth, through Sunday, the twenty-first. In addition, there's a spaghetti feed on Saturday evening."

"It all sounds wonderful. I'm sorry I'm going to miss it this year. Do be sure to remember that e-mail."

"I will, Mrs. Jolly."

"I suppose I should get to my picture taking. I was originally just going to snap a few photos, but I'm so impressed that I think I'll do a full-page spread. I can snap some shots today and then come back tomorrow, when you're open for business. I'd love to get a shot of Zak as Santa."

"I think Zak plans to do the Santa thing from ten to two tomorrow," I informed her. "As long as you're out and about with your camera, you should get some shots of the windows along Main Street. In my opinion Bears and Beavers has the best window this year, although they're all pretty spectacular."

"What a wonderful idea. I haven't had a chance to visit the windows yet this season and it's one of my favorite holiday activities. Thank you for the suggestion."

I turned to watch a large flatbed truck filled with wood pull into the lot. "It looks like Buck is here with the lumber for the snack shack. I really should go and tell him where to leave it. Feel free to wander around and take whatever shots you'd like."

"I will. You know, I may just come back this evening and get a shot of the lights when it's dark. Do you plan to leave them on all night?"

"Levi set them up on a timer. I think they'll go off at eleven each evening. He's staying in the cabin to keep an eye on things because the lot is unsecured. I don't think he wanted the lights shining in the window all night."

"I was wondering how you were going to prevent folks from just walking off with your inventory. I don't suppose you have a water fountain on-site? I usually carry bottled water, but I left it sitting on my kitchen counter."

"There are bottles of water in the refrigerator in the cabin. You can go on in and help yourself."

"Thank you. In spite of all the snow I find the air to be dry this afternoon."

I said my good-byes to Mrs. Jolly and headed over to talk to Buck Stevenson, who was new to Ashton Falls. He'd bought the old lumber mill a while back and was still getting settled in the area. Zak and I had become better acquainted with him when he'd temporarily been a suspect in a murder investigation the previous month. I knew Zak had taken a liking to the man and had been showing him around, introducing him to people, and helping him get involved in the community.

"Afternoon, Buck," I greeted. "If you don't mind pulling your truck around to the front we thought we'd set the snack shack up near the entrance."

"No problem." Buck bent down to pet Charlie, who'd trotted over when he'd seen the man arrive. I'd heard Buck had spent some time in prison for killing a man in a bar fight. Initially, I wasn't certain I could trust him, but Charlie seemed to love him, and my dog was as good a judge of character as anyone I knew.

"It looks like you have a good turnout for the setup party," Buck added.

"Yeah, we were lucky to get so much help. We should be done in no time."

"I was at the lodge last night, and Ethan and a few of the guys mentioned they might stop by to help put the snack shack together as long as Lamé wasn't going to be around."

Principal Lamé had also recently joined the lodge, and in the short time he'd been a member he'd ruffled some feathers due to his tendency to obsess over every little rule and bylaw. Last I'd heard, the entire membership of the men's club was about to lynch the guy. The more I considered this, the more apparent it became that there was a pattern at play. Lamé had been a citizen of Ashton Falls for less than two years, but in that relatively short period of time he'd managed to make quite a few enemies, due mainly, as far as I could tell, to his inclination to need to control and micromanage everything.

"I haven't seen him so far, so I think we're safe," I replied.

"I'm not surprised; the guy doesn't seem to be the dig-in-and-get-his-hands-dirty type. Zak around? I wanted to talk to him about the wood he ordered for Hometown Christmas."

"He went to pick up the sleigh we plan to use for Santa. He should be back anytime."

I turned as I heard a loud crash, followed by raucous laughter. It seemed the boys were having just a tad bit too much fun unloading the trees. Oh, well;

the tree lot was Levi's puppy, so I guessed I'd let him handle any broken branches that might result from the rowdy teens and their approach to the job.

"I was chatting with a couple of the local contractors last night and we thought it would be fun to build Santa a house we could construct in the park," Buck continued. "It would be a temporary structure that could be disassembled and stored every year when it wasn't in use. I understand that last year you set up the event in the community center, but this would provide a dedicated venue for the event each year."

"Have you talked to Willa about it?" I asked.

Willa Walton was the head of the events committee.

"Briefly. She suggested I bring it up at the meeting on Tuesday. If the committee approves it we'll only have a week and a half to get it set up, but with enough help it should really only take a day. Zak seems to have a lot of pull with the committee. I figure if he likes the idea, it should be a slam dunk."

"If it involves extravagant decorations I'm sure he'll be all for it. I'll text him and tell him that you want to talk to him. In the meantime, why don't you pull around to the front and I'll grab a couple of the guys to help us unload."

"I have the invoice." Buck took a piece of paper out of his pocket. "Is it okay if I just drop it off in the cabin?"

"Yeah, that would be fine. There's already a bunch of other paperwork on a table to the right as you walk in, but I'm sure if you put your invoice on top Levi will be sure to see it."

As I walked toward the back of the lot to recruit some of the high school students who were helping Levi, I took a minute to really look around at what we had accomplished. In spite of the fact that Levi was more than a little irritated at having to give up two of his three weeks of Christmas break to sell Christmas trees, he had done a fabulous job pulling everything together. The trees were displayed nicely so you could really get a good look at them, rather than being lumped in a pile, which was what several of the other lots had chosen to do. Holiday music filled the air, and Santa Zak was scheduled to be on-site for two hours every weekday and four hours every weekend afternoon. I was sure that once we got the shack set up, Ellie's cookies, candies, and hot and cold drinks would be popular with both children and adults. And best of all, Mother Nature had cooperated, providing fresh snow as a backdrop to the decorations Zak had spent the entire day putting up. The lot really did have a Christmas Village feel.

"Everything is looking good," I commented to Levi as he handed trees down to the students who were helping from the back of a flatbed truck.

Levi stood up straight and flexed his back. "You can thank Jett and the gang for most of it."

I turned toward Jett and his friends. "Buck is here with the wood for the snack shack," I informed the group. "He could use some help unloading if a couple of you want to head out to the front."

"Jett, you and Tyson head over to help Buck; the rest of you stay here and help me," Levi instructed.

"I probably should grab some clean gloves," Jett said. "These are full of sap. I'd hate to mess up the new wood."

"I put all the extra gloves on the bench in the cabin. You and Tyson can each grab a pair."

"Thanks, Coach." Both boys trotted off.

"Ellie here yet?" Levi asked me.

"Not yet."

"Do you mind calling and asking her to bring a bunch of pizzas? The guys have been working hard. Tell her I'll reimburse her when she gets here."

"I'll call in the order and put it on my credit card," I offered. "Any special requests?"

I immediately realized my mistake when everyone shouted out something different.

"How about I just get a selection? If Ellie can't pick them up for some reason I'll just ask for them to be delivered."

After chatting with Levi for a few more minutes I headed back toward the cabin. I didn't have the phone number for the pizza place on hand, but I remembered seeing a phone book inside. I was halfway to my destination when Zak pulled up with the sleigh. I changed my trajectory to greet him and Bella as they parked in the lot.

"If it isn't Santa Zak and his shaggy brown Santa dog."

Bella, a dark brown Newfoundland mix, was sitting on the seat next to Zak, wearing a Santa hat.

"Maybe we should get some antlers for Charlie," Zak suggested as he hopped down from the sleigh.

"Good idea," I agreed as I kissed Zak on the lips.

"I had to borrow Nellie to get the sleigh over here," Zak told me, referring to the horse who was attached to the front of the sleigh. "I promised to return her right away. I thought I'd grab some food on the way back. Do you want anything?"

"I was just about to call in a pizza order for everyone," I informed him.

"The new pizza place that just opened up is right next to the stable where I need to return Nellie. Go ahead and call in the order and I'll pick everything up after I drop off the horse. I'm going to leave Bella with you."

"Okay," I agreed to the plan. "If I call right now they should be ready by the time you get there."

"Get one with tomatoes and anchovies," Zak requested.

I grimaced. Sometimes Zak had the strangest food preferences.

Zak left with Nellie and I headed toward the cabin once again. I opened the door only to bump into none other than Principal Joe Lamé, lurking just inside the small building.

"Hey, watch where you're going," Lamé spat out when I literally ran into him.

"I'm sorry, but I didn't see you. What are you doing in here?" I asked.

"Looking for Boomer."

Boomer, Levi's new assistant coach, had been the star receiver for the Ashton Falls Bulldogs a few years ago. He'd played for a major college team until he tore up his leg in a motorcycle accident last spring and had to retire from football for good. He'd returned to Ashton Falls a defeated man with an uncertain future until his father had talked Principal Lamé into hiring him as Levi's assistant. The team had done well the previous season without his help, but this year they were unstoppable.

"I think he's unloading trees in the back," I informed the unpleasant man.

"Perhaps I'll just wait here for him. You can run along and do whatever it is you need to be doing."

I hesitated. There was certainly no reason Lamé couldn't wait in the cabin. Still, I found myself reluctant to leave him there alone. "I was actually coming in to warm up." I moved a brown jacket and sat down on one of the benches that surrounded the small dining table. "You can wait with me if you'd like."

I really hoped he wouldn't.

Lamé frowned. He looked out the window and then back at me. His eyes darted around the room, and he seemed agitated and nervous. After several seconds of indecision, he seemed to make up his mind about something. I could tell he wasn't happy about my unwillingness to leave.

"It looks like Boomer is headed this way. I guess I'll head out to meet him. Be sure to close the door when you leave. I found it cracked open. We wouldn't want any raccoons to get inside."

"Will do." I plastered on my best fake smile. "Oh, and don't forget your jacket."

"It isn't mine," Lamé informed me. "Ethan Carlton was leaving the trailer when I came in, so it could be his."

"Okay, I'll just hang it on the hook."

I watched Lamé walk out of the cabin and across the tree lot, where he met up with Boomer. The fact that the two men were so chummy really grated on my nerves. I suppose my discontent could be due to the fact that Boomer seemed to be after Levi's job and Lamé appeared to be more than eager to give it to him, although neither of them had ever said as much in my presence.

As I continued to look out the window, I could see the two men were deep in a serious conversation. Both glanced back toward the cabin several times as they spoke. I have to admit I was curious as to why Lamé and Boomer were meeting at the tree lot, and it was odd that the principal would come inside the cabin rather than head over to the area where the trees were being unloaded. The guys had been making quite a racket as they worked, so it seemed the back of the lot would be the logical place to go to look for someone. I glanced around the interior of the room I was standing in. Nothing appeared to have been disturbed, but there was something about Lamé's startled, somewhat guilty expression when I walked in and caught him here that sent my Zodar tingling. I really hate it when that happens.

Chapter 2

"Love the antlers." Levi yawned when I showed up early the next morning to help him set up for the opening. Based on the fact that he answered the door dressed only in boxer shorts, I was willing to bet he'd still been in bed when I knocked.

"Thanks. Charlie and I match." I nodded toward my adorable dog, who was dressed as Charlie the Red-Nosed Terrier. "I'm glad to see you're still in one piece this morning. I was concerned when you didn't want to leave the bar with Zak, Ellie, and me last night."

Levi shrugged. "A guy I know from work was there alone, so I stayed and had another beer with him."

I gave him my fiercest look of disbelief.

"Okay, so maybe I had a couple of beers, but I knew I wasn't going to be driving because I was staying in the cabin, which was conveniently located just down the street from the bar, and Karloff was staying the night at Ellie's, so he wouldn't be here waiting for me."

"What time did you get in?" I knew I sounded more like Levi's mother than his best friend, but I was becoming concerned by his strange behavior over the past couple of months. It had started around the time he broke up with Darla, a woman he'd been dating for a while, but he hadn't seemed all that into her, so I suspected it had more to do with Lamé's willingness to give Boomer all the credit for the football team's unheard of success in spite of the fact that Levi had been working with the boys for several years now. Levi had first begun working with the team as a summer conditioning trainer while still in college and then got the full-time position when he graduated.

Levi stood up and looked at his watch. "I guess I got in around midnight. It's only eight and we don't open until ten, so I don't see the problem."

"The problem is that if I hadn't shown up to wake you, you'd most likely still be snoring away when the first customers arrived. Think of the scandal there would have been if you'd answered the door in your underwear if it had been Chelsea Manchester or Lizzie Breeland who'd shown up first."

"I wouldn't have answered the door in my underwear if it had been them. You have a very distinctive knock, so I knew it was you before I even opened the door."

"Distinctive knock?"

"Three quick raps followed by a short pause and then two hard knocks."

"Okay, so maybe you did recognize my knock. Still, it seems like you've been hanging out in the bar a lot more lately than you have in the past. Is everything okay?"

Levi shrugged. "Yeah, everything is great."

I doubted it, but I figured this wasn't the time to get into a serious discussion about odd best friend behavior.

"Perhaps you should clean up and get dressed before the others arrive. I'm going to look around to make sure everything's ready. Ellie should be here any minute to drop off the food for the snack shack."

"Zak here?" Levi asked.

"He had a few stops to make, but he'll be here shortly."

Charlie and I decided to get the snack shack opened up in anticipation of Ellie's arrival. The guys had done a wonderful job setting it up. Not only was it completely enclosed so that it could be locked up at night but it had a large wooden window that doubled as an overhang when opened. Ellie had decided that the little shed needed to be brightened up, so we'd spent a good part of the day before painting it to look like a gingerbread house. It really was adorable and I knew the kids would love it.

Levi must have switched on the stereo, which had been set up to play Christmas favorites on a continuous loop. "Here Comes Santa Claus" filled the silence I'd previously been enjoying. Charlie and I made sure the window was secure before we headed toward the back of the lot, where Levi had set up a work shed of sorts to house the wood for the tree stands and the tools needed to assemble them. I'm not sure why, but for some reason something seemed off. I knew it was most likely my imagination. I do tend to have a very active mind, and I often sense a problem where none actually exists. I opened the shed and peeked inside, noticing several of the tools on the floor. I stepped out of the shed and looked around. Nothing appeared to be out of order. Maybe at the end of the day the guys had just tossed the tools in rather than returning them to the hooks Levi had installed.

"Charlie," I called. He'd been trotting along next to me but had suddenly disappeared. "Charlie," I called louder.

I heard a short bark from behind a stack of trees that hadn't as of yet been set up for display. I headed in that direction when Charlie barked again.

"Whatcha doin'?" I asked my little reindeer dog.

Charlie looked up but didn't move toward me.

"Oh, Charlie, not again." I sighed as I noticed two dark brown boots that appeared to be attached to two very human legs sticking out from beneath a pile of branches Levi had saved to make into wreaths.

"Poor Mrs. Jolly," Ellie said as we sat on the front stoop of the cabin and waited for Sheriff Salinger to finish interviewing Levi. Zak had taken Charlie and the other dogs home because Salinger's men were combing every inch of the place. The grand opening of the tree lot had been delayed for one day at least. I just hoped the sheriff would release the property so we could open tomorrow and all the trees Levi and his volunteers had cut wouldn't go to waste.

"Who would kill poor, sweet Mrs. Jolly?" I asked.

"She was always so nice to us when we had her for history," Ellie agreed.

"Of course we were both good students. I suppose if you managed to get on her bad side you might have an entirely different perspective on the woman," I commented. "Did you know she was going to flunk Jett Jarratt? And if he doesn't graduate, he'll lose his chance at a college scholarship. It could change the course of his entire life, and all because he can't remember what year the Second World War started or who was president after Hoover."

"You don't think Jett . . . ?" Ellie asked.

"I hope not. I was just using him as an example to make the point that every student might not like Mrs. Jolly the way we did. Although now that I think about it, Jett did have a pretty good reason to resent her."

Ellie frowned. "Nah. Jett wouldn't do something like that. He's just a kid."

"Yeah, you're right," I agreed. "I don't really see Jett as the violent type, and I certainly can't imagine him killing an old woman over a history grade. To be honest, I can't think of a single person who would want to kill Mrs. Jolly. I suppose Salinger and his men will get it all sorted out."

"Salinger sure has been talking to Levi for a long time."

"He probably thinks Levi is the number-one suspect," I speculated. "He was on the property all night, and Salinger said Mrs. Jolly was hit in the head with a hammer—Levi's hammer, to be exact. And to make matters worse, I already spilled the beans that the hammer was last seen in the cabin. I guess I shouldn't have said as much, but Salinger asked me about it, and I did specifically remember putting it on the counter near the sink after I finished using it yesterday. Whoever killed Mrs. Jolly has to have had access to the cabin."

"Let me guess: Levi has the only key."

"As far as I know."

"The property belongs to Jett's dad," Ellie pointed out. "I'd be willing to bet Mr. Jarratt has an extra key to the cabin. Maybe even more than one. If Jett wanted to get into the cabin, it seems like he'd be able to find a way to do so."

"I thought we didn't think Jett could have done such a thing," I pointed out.

"I know that's what we said, but if there are only two suspects, Levi and Jett, then I'm going to have to go with Jett as the killer," Ellie decided.

"Oh my god," I gasped. "I mentioned to Zak in front of Jett and some of the other guys that Mrs. Jolly loved his lights and planned to come back after dark to take some more photos. If Jett wanted to get rid of his one roadblock to a spectacular future, he had the perfect opportunity to do it. I know Levi mentioned to the guys that he was going out to dinner with us, so Jett would have known the place would be deserted for several hours."

Ellie bit her lip. She turned to look at me. "I know what I said about suspecting Jett over Levi, but do you really think he could have done something so gruesome? Hitting someone over the head with a hammer seems so personal."

"I'm having a hard time believing Jett could be our killer," I answered honestly, "but he does have a lot riding on being able to graduate in the spring. Desperate people are sometimes driven to desperate acts."

"Yeah, but why would he break into the cabin to get Levi's hammer? If Jett came back last night to confront Mrs. Jolly, it seems it would have been easier to bring a weapon and wait for her outside in the shadows," Ellie pointed out.

"True. Unless he was intentionally trying to frame Levi, but that doesn't seem likely. Jett and the guys really like him."

"There were a lot of people in and out of the cabin yesterday," Ellie said. "Anyone could have taken the hammer after you put it on the counter."

"True, but I didn't notice anyone walking around with it."

"Someone could have taken it and then stashed it somewhere on the property."

"Why would anyone do that?" I asked.

"I don't know. It's just a possibility that means Levi and Jett aren't the only people with opportunity. Do you remember seeing the hammer later in the day?"

I thought about Ellie's question. I tried to remember if it was still on the counter when I went inside to call for the pizzas. I remembered looking for the phone book, but that had been on the desk. The counter would have been out of my line of vision the entire time I was in the cabin, and I never returned to the kitchen for any reason because Zak brought beverages, paper plates, and napkins along with the pizza.

"I wasn't looking for it, so I didn't notice if it was still on the counter when we locked up before going to the bar," I said, "but you're correct that there were people in and out of the building throughout the day. I know Chelsea went inside to deliver a box of ornaments, I offered Mrs. Jolly a bottle of water from the fridge, Buck dropped off his invoice for the wood, Jett and Tyson went in to get gloves, and Principal

Lamé was in the cabin just standing around when I went in to order the pizza. Oh," I added, "and Ethan Carlton left his coat inside. That's a lot of people, and those are only the ones I know about. I'm sure once we point that out to Salinger, he'll see that anyone could have taken Levi's hammer."

"Yeah, I guess." Ellie looked toward the cabin door. I knew she was worried. Salinger had arrested Levi once before with a lot less evidence than he seemed to currently have.

"Don't worry. If Salinger gets the lame idea to arrest Levi again I'll have Zak get him a lawyer who'll have him out before lunch."

"It seems like Zak should be back from taking the dogs home by now," Ellie said.

"Yeah, that's what I was thinking. He might have taken them for a quick run. Salinger isn't known for his speedy interrogations; Zak most likely realized we could be here for hours. Maybe I should have asked him to bring us back something to eat."

"I brought doughnuts if you want." Ellie offered me a white paper bag.

"Coffee?" I said hopefully.

"Sorry. I figured we could just make coffee in the coffee maker inside. If I'd have known..."

I opened the bag and took out a glazed doughnut. The bakery in town made wonderfully soft doughnuts that tended to melt in your mouth, and the glaze they used was just the right amount of sweet. I felt my tension ebb just a bit as I took my second bite.

"You should have one," I suggested. "They're delicious."

"I ate two on the way over," Ellie confessed. "If I knew that stress eating was going to be the order of the day I would have waited."

I finished my first doughnut and started in on a second. "By the way, did you ever find that turnover recipe you were looking for?" I realize discussing recipes wasn't the most urgent matter at hand, but Ellie looked pale and I wanted to get her mind off Levi and his possible involvement in the murder of Mrs. Jolly. Ellie had been looking for a recipe her friend Teri had sent her for pumpkin turnovers. She'd thought she'd put the recipe in her computer file, but when she went to retrieve it she couldn't locate it.

"Zak found it," Ellie informed me. "I'm not sure what happened, but it ended up in some random folder on the backup drive rather than on the desktop. If Zak hadn't done a search for me, I never would have found it."

"And are they as good as you hoped?"

"Even better," Ellie answered. "I'm going to make them to sell at Ellie's Beach Hut over the winter. Zak also came across a recipe my friend Karen sent me for shortbread. I'm going to make it this week. It's fun to try out new recipes for the holiday."

"I'm still dreaming about the cinnamon rolls your mom made last year at Christmas. They were some of the best I've ever had."

"She used a recipe her friend Dawn gave her a few years ago at a pastry party she went to over Thanksgiving weekend."

"Pastry party?" I asked. Whatever it was, it sounded delicious.

"It's like a cookie exchange only with pastries. Mom is involved with a group of cooks who share recipes."

"Sounds like fun."

"Maybe we should organize our own cookie exchange this year," Ellie suggested. "We can open it up to include all types of cookies, candies, and pastries. It'll be a fun way to try out other people's recipes."

"I'm in as long as I can bring slice-and-bake cookies from the refrigerator aisle."

Ellie looked at me sadly. "The keyword here is *recipe*. I'm sure you can come up with something. How about those rum balls your grandmother used to make? They were really good."

"She got the recipe from her cousin Stefani, but I can see if Pappy knows where Grandma's old recipe box is. If not, I can e-mail Stefani to ask her if she still has the recipe. I guess it would be fun to make something Grandma always made for the holidays when I was growing up. Our search for the potato cheese soup recipe last Christmas really helped me feel close to her during the time of year that was always her favorite. We can have the exchange at Zak's since there's plenty of room. Who else should we invite?"

"We should start a list. I'm thinking maybe a dozen women would be a good number. We can ask everyone to bring enough cookies to exchange with everyone else, as well as enough copies of the printed recipes so that everyone can take one with them. I've been dying to get Lisa's recipe for potato candy, so maybe if we invite her, she can be persuaded to bring the candy as her offering."

"Oh, and Vivian's candied cherry slices," I added. My mouth was beginning to water at the thought of so many holiday treats.

"Now I'm hungry again." Ellie grabbed the bag of doughnuts from my hand and selected a chocolate glazed. "I seem to be hungry all the time lately. I'm not sure what that's all about. I never eat three doughnuts in one day."

"It's a good thing you got a full dozen," I said as I reached for my third. Ellie and I were going to need to go shopping for bigger pants if we weren't careful.

"Is Scooter still coming for the holiday?" Ellie asked as she licked the frosting from her fingers.

Scooter Sherwood is a precocious nine-year-old Zak had befriended when I asked him to run interference with his father concerning a dog bite. The father had been willing to drop his complaint if Zak agreed to babysit Scooter while he was out of town. Zak and Scooter had hit it off and the two had become close friends. Zak had even taken on a sort of mentoring role with the boy, enrolling him in boarding school on the East Coast after his father had dumped him off on his grandparents.

I nodded. "He'll be here a week from today, and he's bringing a friend with him."

"Zak mentioned that. I can't believe the kid's parents would abandon him over Christmas. Talk about cold and uncaring."

"According to Scooter, his friend's parents are anthropologists or archeologists or something like that. Anyway, they're in Egypt, or maybe it was Peru."

"Egypt or Peru? Those are pretty different places," Ellie said.

"I guess I wasn't really paying attention when Zak was telling me about it. I just know they aren't able to leave the dig for even a short break and there's some sort of problem with having Alex join them this year. It seems Alex has traveled all over the world, joining his parents for short visits when he's on school break, but this time the government wouldn't allow him to come, or maybe it was too dangerous for a nine-year-old. I can't remember."

"You really need to pay more attention when your fiancé tells you things," Ellie scolded.

"Yeah, I guess I do. When Zak first told me that we were going to have the two boys for three weeks I guess my brain shorted out until I was able to digest the situation. I have to admit I wasn't entirely thrilled with the idea, but the more I thought about it, the more I realized it would be a good opportunity for Zak and me to do something memorable for two kids who don't have attentive adults in their lives."

"It's nice that you and Zak are willing to open your home to them. And if you need a babysitter, just ask. Kids and Christmas really do go together. It's times like this that I miss having a child of my own."

"It'll happen." I squeezed Ellie's hand in support.

"I know. And Shep and I have big plans of our own for the holiday."

I looked into the white bag and decided that one more doughnut really couldn't hurt. I had a busy week ahead, I reasoned. I was certain I'd burn it off . . . I hoped.

"Why don't you and Shep plan to come for Christmas Eve dinner?" I invited. "Mom, Dad, and Harper are going to come over, and I'm planning to ask Pappy and Hazel. We'll have Levi and Karloff as well. It'll be fun."

"Okay, I'm in. Can I bring something?"

"I guess you should ask Zak about that. He was talking about making lasagna, but I don't think it's a for-sure thing. I know he wants to make something he can cook ahead so he can relax with the family rather than spending the evening in the kitchen."

"Lasagna is good for that," Ellie agreed. "You can assemble it the day before and then bake it the day of. Add some salad and garlic bread and you have an inviting meal. Maybe I'll offer to bring dessert. I have a recipe for boiled custard that I got from my friend Debra that I've been wanting to try out. I'll bring some of the cookies I get from the exchange too. I bet your parents are excited about Harper's first Christmas."

Harper is my adorable eight-month-old sister.

"They really are, especially Mom. She's been shopping for a first Christmas bib, first Christmas jammies, and, of course, a special first Christmas stocking. And the dress she got her to wear to Christmas services is absolutely adorable. She's definitely going to be the best-dressed baby in town."

"And has big sis been shopping for little sis as well?" Ellie asked.

I grinned. "Oh, yeah. Shopping for a baby is so much fun. It's like playing with doll clothes. I'll probably have to take out a loan against my truck to pay for everything, but I've been having the best time. I saw this adorable outfit with a reindeer sweater online that I think I'm going to have to get. This is the first year that either Mom or I have had a baby to shop for, and we're both going a little crazy."

"I keep forgetting your mom wasn't around for your first Christmas," Ellie said.

"It's a little weird for me, but I love having her in my life, even if she was twenty-five years late to the party. I think now that she sees how fulfilling being a mother can be, she regrets the decisions she made in the past."

"I'm sure she does."

"It looks like the crime scene unit has found something." I nodded toward the rear of the lot, where the men had gathered and were all standing around looking at something.

"I wonder what they found."

"I don't know, but they seem pretty excited about it," I commented.

One of the men separated from the others. He walked toward Ellie and me with something clutched in his hand. It looked like a Serenity High School beanie. The football team had sold them as a fund-raiser in the fall, and a lot of people in town had one just like it.

"Do either of you recognize this?" the deputy asked.

Ellie and I looked at the blood-soaked hat and then at each other. While the beanie could have belonged to anyone in town, the Coach of the Year pin on the side of it could only be Levi's.

Chapter 3

By Tuesday the hoopla created by Mrs. Jolly's death had died down to a simmer. It seemed odd to me that life could return to normal quite as easily as it had. Salinger had interviewed everyone who might have seen anything, as well as most of the people who were present at the tree lot at any point on Friday. Levi was cleared once it was determined that Mrs. Jolly had been killed around nine p.m.; he had been at the bar until well after midnight.

It seemed that Mrs. Jolly had lived a very unspectacular life. Although she went by the name *Mrs.* Jolly, she was never actually married and had no children. And while she was friendly enough, she didn't seem to have any real friends. The other teachers at the high school reported that while she was liked by most, she didn't seek companionship outside of work hours and turned down any invitations she was offered to participate in parties, baby showers, or other events. She'd been popular with some of her students but very unpopular with others. According to the short obituary in the local paper, she'd lived alone in a small one-bedroom house without even a pet to keep her company.

Principal Lamé hired a substitute to take over Mrs. Jolly's classes until a new teacher could be found. Most of her students had returned to studying for finals and making plans for winter break, and few, if any, spent time mourning the woman who had briefly touched their lives.

"I feel so bad for Mrs. Jolly," I said to Ellie when I arrived at Rosie's a few minutes early for the weekly events committee meeting.

"I know what you mean. As far as I know, no one is even putting together a service. It's like she was never even a part of our community. Everyone is just going about their business like nothing happened."

"I keep trying to remember that poem that goes something like 'since he never really lived they claimed he never died.' Or maybe it's a song. I'm not sure."

"I think it's a poem," Ellie said. "Although I've seen a bunch of different versions. I don't really know where it came from."

It was in the back of my mind that there was a poster displayed somewhere in town with the poem, but for the life of me I couldn't place it. I hate when I have a memory that hangs just at the edge of my consciousness and I know I know something but can't quite figure out how to access it.

"Maybe we should organize something. A memorial of some type," I suggested after I decided to give up trying to remember the poem.

"I think that would be nice. I'll help you put something together. Maybe for this weekend."

"Actually, this weekend isn't good," I told her. "Scooter is coming, and I've already told Levi I'd help him with the new grand opening of the tree lot, which is scheduled for Saturday. Maybe we can just write something up and ask Pastor Dan to read it at church on Sunday."

"That's a good idea."

"What's a good idea?" Levi asked as he sat down next to Ellie.

"We were talking about doing some type of memorial service for Mrs. Jolly, and Zoe suggested having Dan read something at church on Sunday," Ellie filled him in.

"You worked with her. Do you know anything about her life other than the fact that she was a teacher at the high school for a lot of years?" I asked Levi.

"Not really. She was nice enough, but she tended to keep to herself. I know she took over as newspaper adviser when Patty went out on maternity leave. I suppose we can talk to the newspaper staff. They spent more time with her than her history students."

"Are you talking about Holly Jolly?" Hazel asked as she walked into the room with Willa.

"Yeah. We were thinking about putting together something for the Sunday service. A memorial of sorts," I answered.

"I'd like to help," Hazel offered. "I didn't know the woman well, but she did come into the library every week, and she'd usually stop and chat for a few minutes. I don't know much about her, but I will say she had a voracious appetite for the written word."

"We're having a hard time figuring out who her friends might have been," Ellie said. "None of us really knew her all that well, and it would be nice to find someone she was closer to, to say a few words at the service."

Hazel frowned. "I have to say, not a single person comes to mind."

"You know what's so odd," Ellie added, "Mrs. Jolly was . . . well, jolly. She always seemed to be in a good mood and she always remembered your name and all the little details of your life. She seemed like such a friendly, outgoing woman. How is it that we can't think of a single person who really knew her? She lived and worked in this town for most of her life. She has to have had friends. Neighbors? *Someone* who cared about her."

"I can ask around at the high school," Levi offered. "I'll post a notice that we want to do some sort of service and ask that anyone who has any anecdotes or stories should contact one of us."

"Let's put something in the paper as well," I suggested. "I don't have a superbusy day today, so I'll go talk to her closest neighbors. I'll see if Zak can help me."

"I'm always happy to help you in any way I can," Zak said as he walked in with Buck, Paul Iverson, and my dad, Hank Donovan.

"We're trying to put together some type of a memorial service for Mrs. Jolly," I explained. "The problem is that no one seems to know anything about her other than that she was a teacher at the high school. I thought we could talk to her neighbors."

"Have they figured out who killed her?" Paul asked.

"Not as far as I know. I'm pretty sure now that Salinger has managed to clear Levi, he's clean out of suspects."

"This is just too sad." Willa shook her head.

"What are we talking about?" Gilda Reynolds asked as she walked in.

"Mrs. Jolly," I said.

"It's such a tragedy. She seemed to be such a friendly sort."

"I don't suppose you know anything about her personal life?" I asked. "Friends, hobbies, accomplishments? Anything we can use to come up with a eulogy."

"Sorry; I didn't really know her," Gilda answered.

"I know we're supposed to be talking about Hometown Christmas, but suddenly I'm finding it hard to find the Christmas spirit," Hazel commented. "It's beginning to sound like this poor woman lived in our town for most of her life but was never really made a part of the community. It's just so incredibly sad."

"Not joining in must have been her choice," Levi pointed out.

"Maybe," Hazel acknowledged, "but people who isolate themselves usually have a reason for doing so, and most times that reason is sad."

I sighed as I thought of the woman I didn't really know very well but knew I'd somehow miss.

"While we may not feel like talking about Hometown Christmas, it starts in nine days, so we do need to get on topic," Willa announced, effectively ending the conversation. The ability to take control of a meeting when control is what's needed was what made Willa a great group leader. "Let's start with a presentation by Zak and Buck concerning the proposed Santa house."

The meeting went a lot longer than usual, given the fact that we'd gotten a late start and had a lot to discuss. Zak and I talked about visiting Mrs. Jolly's closest neighbors but decided to call ahead and make the visits the following morning. Zak was able to locate Mrs. Jolly's address on the Internet, so it wasn't difficult to figure out who we needed to set up appointments with. Luckily, I knew the women who lived on either side of her, and thankfully, both were willing to meet with Zak and me in the morning.

I didn't get to the Zoo until noon, but Jeremy and Tiffany had everything under control. They'd even managed to find homes for most of the cats we'd taken in when the Cat Lady of Ashton Falls died before Thanksgiving. Traditionally, the holiday season was a slow time of year for the shelter. Most of the wild animals that live in our area are tucked in for the winter, and very few people drop off unwanted pets just prior to Christmas. In addition, the number of people looking to adopt pets is greatly increased as the Christmas wishes of the town's children clamor to be met.

"How'd the meeting go?" Jeremy asked as I stomped the snow off my boots and hung up my jacket.

"Really good. It looks like Santa will have his own house in the park this year. Zak, Buck, and a few other volunteers are already putting it together. I'm really glad the committee approved it because Zak had already gone ahead and bought the wood. I have a feeling if the Santa house wasn't approved for the park it would have ended up in our front yard."

"Is Zak going crazy with the decorations again?"

"Not as much as he did at Halloween. He's been pretty busy with other things. Scooter is coming this weekend, so he's been working really hard getting all his clients taken care of." Zak is a software developer in very high demand. "He's also been a lot more involved with the setup for Hometown Christmas than he was last year. Between that and helping Levi get the tree lot ready, his schedule has been full."

"What's going to happen to all the trees now that Salinger has closed the lot?"

"Actually, we've been given the go-ahead to reopen at the end of the week. Levi decided to wait until school was out for break, so the new grand opening will be on Saturday."

"Has Salinger figured out who killed Mrs. Jolly?" Jeremy asked.

"Not so far, but he said he's about done with the lot in any event. I find the whole thing really sad. The more I look into her life, the more I realize that Mrs. Jolly didn't seem to have one. At least as measured by most people's standards. I mean, she had a job and she visited the library and shopped at the market, but she didn't seem to have any friends or activities outside of work as far as I can tell. She didn't even have a pet. I can't imagine living alone and not having a dog or cat to come home to."

"There are a lot of people who don't want the bother or expense of a pet," Jeremy pointed out. "In fact, only a few of my single friends have one. None of the guys in the band has a pet, in spite of the fact that I've tried to talk several of them into adopting at one time or another. Pets require a commitment a lot of people don't want to make."

"That's just because they don't know what they're missing. I can't imagine a life without my four-legged housemates. It just seems like it would be so empty to live all alone. Have you ever heard that poem that says something about not dying because you never really lived?"

"There's a framed poster on the wall in the insurance office," Jeremy informed me. "It features a poem with a theme like the one you're referring to."

"That's where I've seen it," I realized. "I've had the last couple of lines rattling around in my head all day, but I couldn't remember the rest of it or where I'd seen it. I don't suppose you remember the rest of it? It had something to do with not taking risks in life, but I can't remember the exact words."

Jeremy thought about it. "I think it goes something like this:

> "There was a very cautious man
> Who never laughed or played.
> He never risked, he never tried,
> He never sang or prayed.
> And when one day he passed away,
> His insurance was denied.
> For since he never really lived,
> They claimed he never really died."

"How can you remember that?" I asked.

"I'm a musician." Jeremy shrugged. "I tend to remember lyrics. Poems are just songs without the melody."

"Yeah, I guess that's true."

Socrates, one of the cats we'd rescued the previous month but had yet to place, jumped up onto the counter in front of me and began to purr. I ran my hands through his long fur, enjoying the comfort provided by the steady rhythm of his internal motor. "I suppose it's a little late at this point to do much about the fact that Mrs. Jolly seemed to have been a forgotten citizen in our community, but I'm not going to let her murder turn into some long-forgotten cold case. Maybe she never really lived, but she sure as heck really died. A very real person killed her and I'm going to find out who it was."

"Are there any clues at all?" Jeremy asked.

"Not really. We think whoever killed her had to have had access to the cabin at the tree lot because both Levi's hammer and his cap were found at the crime scene. I personally remember putting the hammer on the kitchen counter, and Levi swears he had the beanie on Friday morning but took it off when it began to warm up and left it in the cabin. Someone had to have taken it and left it for the cops to find. The lock to the cabin didn't appear to have been tampered with, so we're assuming that someone either took the items before Levi locked up to go to the bar or had a key. While it's possible that someone walked off with the hammer and cap earlier in the day, we think it's more likely the killer accessed the cabin after we left for dinner. Levi has one key to the cabin, and as far as we know, the only other one is in Tom Jarratt's possession."

"What about the previous tenants?" Jeremy asked.

Socrates butted his head up under my hand when I stopped petting him. He continued to walk back and forth under my arm until I resumed my prior activity.

I will say one thing for the large and slightly overweight tabby: he knew what he wanted and how to get it.

"You know, that's a really good point," I said. "If the locks weren't changed after the antiques store closed, there could be a lot of folks out there with keys. Former employees, the cleaning service, repair personnel. We really have no idea how many keys might have been handed out or who they might have been given to."

"I know the building is for sale," Jeremy added. "I'd be willing to bet the Realtor has a key. There might even have been a lockbox on the property before Levi temporarily moved in."

"I guess I should see if I can find out whether the lock was changed after the antiques store moved out. Figuring out how many people might have keys could help narrow things down, but I'm not sure it will wind up pointing us in a direction. What we really need to do is figure out who had motive to kill Mrs. Jolly and take it from there."

"It doesn't seem like that would be a very long list," Jeremy commented.

"It's not. So far the only person I've been able to identify with a real motive is Jett Jarratt. Mrs. Jolly told me he was flunking her class, and if he didn't get his grades up he wouldn't be graduating in the spring, which would mean bye-bye football scholarship. The thing is that it appears whoever killed Mrs. Jolly intentionally set up Levi, and it seems like Jett really likes him. I'm having a hard time picturing him as the killer."

"What we really need is to find someone with a grudge against both Mrs. Jolly and Levi."

I picked up Socrates and held him to my chest. He was so sweet and loved to cuddle, but the cat was a porker. He had to weigh at least twenty pounds. Jeremy had been monitoring his food intake, as well as making sure he was let out of his cage to get some exercise as often as possible. I had to admit I was growing fond of the beast. He had the sweetest face, which seemed to demand that you love him. If I didn't already have two very demanding kitties at home I'd probably adopt him myself.

"It has to be someone connected to the high school," I realized. "A teacher, student, parent? As far as I know, the high school is the only link between Levi and Mrs. Jolly. I have a feeling that finding the killer is going to be about as easy as finding a needle in a haystack."

"Maybe not. Whoever killed Mrs. Jolly probably knew she was going to be at the lot that evening. Who, other than yourself, knew she was going to take photos of the lights?" Jeremy asked.

I stopped to think about it. There hadn't been anyone around when we were talking that morning; at least not anyone I remembered seeing. Of course, with all the trees it would have been easy for someone to get close enough to eavesdrop without being noticed. Still, there were a lot of people in the area, so the likelihood of someone skulking in the shadows and not being noticed by anyone was slim.

"I mentioned to Zak in front of a bunch of the guys from the team that Mrs. Jolly loved his lights and planned to come back for additional photographs," I shared. "Other than Jett, I'm not really sure who was close enough to hear what I said. Maybe Tyson. He seems to stick to Jett's side like glue most of the time. I guess I should talk to Jett and the guys to see if any of them know anything. I know Salinger talked to everyone who was at the lot on Friday, but maybe I can get someone to say something they might not have told a cop."

"You might be getting into dicey territory interviewing minors without their parents' consent," Jeremy reminded me.

"So I won't interview them. Levi is having a party for the team after school on Friday. The party is the main reason he wanted to wait until Saturday to open the tree lot. Ellie is providing the food for the event. No one will think a thing of it if I show up to help out, and if I happen to have a conversation with one or more of the team members present, who's to say that it's any more than just that? A casual conversation that's in no way an interrogation."

"You're sneaky, Zoe Donovan."

"The sneakiest."

Chapter 4

As it turned out, I had to go to speak to Mrs. Jolly's neighbors alone. Zak had intended to accompany me, but he got a call from one of his clients just as we were walking out the door. Zak is working hard to handle everything from Ashton Falls so he won't have to travel this month, so I was more than happy to let him take care of what he needed to attend to. The previous December Zak had been out of town for most of the month and had missed everything special about the Christmas season. Well, almost everything. We'd managed to carve out a pretty spectacular Christmas Eve and Christmas Day.

Mrs. Jolly lived in a small place in a middle-class neighborhood that had been built by a contractor in the late seventies featuring tidy but unimaginative houses. While this particular area had never been one of my favorites due to the cookie-cutter houses, the people who lived there seemed to like it, few of them moving away once they were settled. Many of the residents were the original owners of the homes, so the neighborhood tended to have an older population, and the people on either side of Mrs. Jolly were widows in their sixties. I decided to visit Erma Olsen first because I knew her the best. Erma had been a nurse in the hospital until she'd retired the previous summer. Charlie and I are frequent visitors to the hospital, and she and I had developed a friendship of sorts while performing Charlie's therapy dog duties.

"Zoe, do come in. Where's Charlie? I hoped you'd bring him."

"I wasn't sure he'd be welcome in all the homes I planned to visit, so I left him home with Zak."

"I've missed you both so much since I retired. You'll have to come to visit again and bring the little guy."

"I will," I promised.

"I've made us some tea. Why don't we take it into the living room?"

I followed Erma down the hall to the back of the house. The main living area was compact but nicely furnished and spotlessly clean. There was a small Christmas tree in one corner and the mantel above the fireplace was decorated with red candles and green fir branches. Other than that, the house seemed to be free of holiday clutter.

Erma showed me to the sofa, where she'd arranged a tray on the coffee table that was situated between it and two wingback chairs. The view from her living room window was spectacular.

"I love your view," I commented. "A lot of homes have so many trees that the view of the summit is blocked completely."

"The view is the main reason I purchased this particular house," Erma said. "I like to watch the storms roll in from the valley, and this lot was situated perfectly to allow me to do just that."

Erma poured the tea she had prepared into china cups.

"So you're here to ask about Holly," she began.

I'd decided to start the conversation talking about the memorial service Ellie and I were putting together with Dan's help and only bring up the murder investigation if it seemed necessary and the situation presented itself. I explained what sort of information we were looking for and why we wanted it.

"Even though Holly and I were neighbors for over thirty years, we weren't close. We'd chat from time to time if we both pulled up in the drive at the same time and had a few longer conversations when we both happened to be out in our gardens. I knew a bit about her life, but not all that much. Holly was a very quiet woman who liked to keep to herself, and I always worked odd hours at the hospital, so much of the time I was sleeping while the rest of the world was awake."

I took a sip of the tea Erma had served. It was surprisingly good. Normally, I'm not a huge tea drinker, preferring coffee when I want something hot, but Erma's tea had a nice flavor, with a bit of a kick.

"This is good," I complimented. "What kind is it?"

"Spiced chai. It's a special blend I buy from a supplier in the valley. I really enjoy the unique flavor."

I set my cup down and focused on the woman across from me. "I know you said you weren't good friends with Holly, but did you ever notice anyone else visiting her on a regular basis?"

Erma appeared to be thinking about it. "I know Lotty Smothers, her neighbor to the east, used to take care of her plants when Holly was out of town. I wouldn't say they were great friends, but she tended to visit more often than I did. Other than that, I really can't say I saw anyone at her place. Again, though, I often worked at night and slept during the day."

"Did you ever see any cars parked in front of her house or anyone coming or going?"

"You know, there *was* someone, now that I think about it. I believe he was a teacher at the high school as well. I can't say I know his name, but he drove a blue Cadillac the times I saw him visiting Holly. The car was an older model; I'd say at least forty years old. I'm afraid I can't tell you what the man looked like, but I definitely remember the car."

I made a mental note to ask Levi about the Caddy.

"Had he been by recently?" I asked.

"I remember seeing the car parked in front of Holly's over the summer, but I don't believe I've seen it since school started."

"Is there anything else at all you can tell me?"

Erma shrugged. "I know Holly moved to Ashton Falls as a young woman, when she got the job teaching at the high school. She never married and she mentioned at one point that she didn't have any family. She liked to knit. Oh, and read. I've never met anyone who read as much as she did. I'd see her come in with a bagful of books at least once a week. I suppose she had a lot of time on her hands."

"Yeah, it sounds like she did. Did she ever have students come by?"

"Not that I can remember. She did have a friendly relationship with the mailman who retired recently— Mr. Hanover. I'd notice her giving him cookies from time to time. I don't believe she'd struck up a similar relationship with the new guy who took over the route."

I made a mental note to visit Mr. Hanover. I'd been meaning to stop in to see how he was doing with the kittens he'd adopted at Halloween.

"I know you said you weren't home very often during the day when you worked as a nurse, but have you noticed anything odd going on since you've retired?"

"Odd?"

"Anyone lurking around the neighborhood?"

"You think whoever killed Holly was stalking her?"

"Not really," I hedged. "I just wanted to be sure to cover all the bases."

Erma appeared to be considering my question. "No, I can't think of a single incident."

After I spoke a while longer to Erma I headed over to Lotty Smothers's. I didn't know her as well as I did Erma, but she was a customer at Donovan's, the store my dad owns and operates, so we were acquaintances. Lotty, like Erma, was a widow, but she was at least a decade younger and closer, I imagined, to Holly Jolly's age.

Unlike Erma's home, which was at least somewhat decorated for the holiday, Lotty's showed not a trace of the season. The house was laid out in a similar floor plan, but the furniture was older and much more worn, and there were distinct traces of dust on most of the wood surfaces. Lotty greeted me warmly and asked me to come in. Her sofa was covered in cat hair, which made me feel right at home.

"So what can I do for you?" Lotty asked after I'd taken a seat.

I explained about the memorial service and my desire to learn what I could about the woman who had been murdered.

"I noticed you were speaking to Erma before coming over here. I'm sure she told you that Holly tended to keep to herself. She was always friendly when we crossed paths, but she never really sought me out, if you know what I mean."

I did.

"I think she was shy," Lotty added.

I thought about the woman who had called me little Zoe Donovan and then hugged me to her ample bosom just the previous week. She sure hadn't seemed shy. Of course, her boisterous behavior could very well be a cover for insecurity and a lack of social confidence. Sometimes those who were the most outwardly extroverted were the most introverted inside.

"Erma mentioned Holly had a visitor over the summer who drove a blue Caddy. Do you know who that might have been?"

"His name is Lou. He's a teacher at the high school. I think they might have been working on a project together."

I realized she was most likely referring to the math teacher, Lou Barton.

"Can you think of any other visitors she might have had?"

"Mr. Hanover used to stop by from time to time to have a cup of coffee or a nice hot cookie. Oh, and there was that young man with the shaggy blond hair who came by from time to time."

"A young man?"

"I don't know his name, but he had an Ashton Falls letterman's jacket. I think he might have graduated a year, maybe two years ago."

"Do you know why he came to see her?" I asked.

"I don't know for certain, but I imagine it was for tutoring. It did seem odd that he came to the house, though. I know she tutored other students, but I believe she met them at the school."

I smiled as a small white cat jumped into my lap. She was such a dainty little thing, not much larger than a kitten, although I could tell she was several years old.

"Did Mrs. Jolly ever mention a hometown?"

"No, she never spoke about her past. I once asked her where she went to college and all she would say was back east. I've never met anyone who was as careful not to share any personal information as she was."

I scratched the cat behind the ears and she started to purr. There really is nothing better than the sound of a contented kitty.

"Erma said you have a key to Holly's place. Do you think it would be possible to look around a bit?"

Lotty hesitated.

"I'm hoping it will give me some insight into the woman. I'm really having a hard time coming up with something I can use for her eulogy. It would be such a shame if she passed from our community without us knowing anything about the woman who shared our space for several decades."

"I guess it wouldn't hurt for you to look around a bit," Lotty decided. "I should go with you, though. I'm not sure it would be proper to just hand over the key."

"Of course. I'll just wait here while you fetch it."

I set the small cat down as soon as Lotty returned with the key. The trip between the two houses was a short one. Lotty chose a route from the back door of her home to the back door of Holly's. Like Erma's house, Mrs. Jolly's was small, compact, and neat as a pin. The big difference between the two was that Mrs. Jolly had every Christmas decoration imaginable on display. It looked as if the holiday had exploded in the living room. There were Santa rugs on the floor, knickknacks on the mantel, garlands around the windows, and a huge tree with dozens of wrapped gifts beneath it. She even had holiday mugs and dishes on display in the kitchen and snowman soap and matching hand towels in the bathroom.

"Wow. I guess Mrs. Jolly really liked Christmas," I commented.

"She'd start decorating right after Halloween," Lotty confirmed. "I'm pretty sure at least half of the storage space in her garage was taken up with holiday decorations."

"If Mrs. Jolly didn't have many friends who are all the gifts for?" I nodded toward the tree.

"She took gifts down to the preschool and made sure every child had one. She also gave a bunch of gifts to the local church to hand out to families in need. Holly really did love Christmas, and she loved children of all ages."

Something just wasn't adding up. How could a woman with such a big heart not have any close friendships? And why would a woman who loved children never have any of her own?

As I walked around the house, which was cluttered with books as well as decorations, I began to form an impression of a woman who lived on the fringe of the reality the rest of us cohabitated in. Sure, she showed up at work, and she gave of herself to those in her life, but she never accepted the friendship I imagined she desperately wanted in return. Why?

"If Mrs. Jolly had sought to have a closer friendship with you would you have been interested?"

"Certainly," Lotty answered. "I invited her over dozens of times, to share a cup of tea or a meal, but she always politely declined. She claimed to be too busy, but she never really did anything other than read and knit."

"And when you did speak to each other, in the garden or whatever, what did you talk about?"

"Mainly the weather, or the insect problem if we were gardening. Most of the time she'd chat for a few minutes and then make an excuse to go inside."

"Erma told me that you had the key to water the plants and keep an eye on the place when she was gone. How often was she away?"

"She left for four weeks every July. Other than that she didn't travel at all."

I looked around the room. There were no photographs, trophies, awards, or any other items that could be linked to a specific person. The room was wildly decorated but impersonal.

"Do you know where she went?" I wondered.

"She never said, and frankly, I never asked. Like I said, she wasn't one to share."

"Mrs. Jolly mentioned to me that she was going to be out of town during Hometown Christmas. Did she speak to you about watching her house while she was gone?"

Lotty shook her head. "She didn't say a word, but if she was only going to be gone for the weekend she wouldn't need me to water plants or pick up mail. It's odd that she planned to be away then, though. She mentioned several times that Christmas was her favorite time of year and that she felt lucky to live in a town that celebrated to the extent that Ashton Falls always did."

There was a stack of mail on the kitchen counter that I quickly sorted through. There were bills and advertisements, but not a single letter or Christmas card. I opened a few drawers to find an assortment of utensils, but nothing that could in any way be considered personal. I'd heard that she borrowed books from the library on a regular basis, but as far as I could tell she didn't own a single book. There were no handwritten notes lying about or messages on an answering machine. Other than her clothing, which was utilitarian, it almost seemed that you could lift her out of the small home and replace her with someone else entirely.

The bathroom cabinet was void of prescriptions, the bedroom of personal mementos. How could a person live in the same house for thirty-odd years and never collect a single thing that announced to the world that the space was hers?

After leaving Lotty's house I decided to drop in on Mr. Hanover. I didn't have his phone number so I couldn't call ahead, but I did know where he lived. He'd said the last time I ran into him that I should stop by sometime and visit the brothers he'd adopted, and it seemed to me that now was as good a time as any to do just that.

Unlike the neighborhood I'd just left, Mr. Hanover lived in one filled with custom houses, each with its own personality. Mr. Hanover's was decorated for the holiday with colored lights and a large evergreen wreath on the door. I wished I had Charlie with me. Mr. Hanover loved Charlie and Charlie loved him. I'd have to stop by another time so the two of them could visit.

"Zoe, how nice to see you. Come in, come in," he invited. "Did you decide to take me up on my offer to visit the boys?"

"You know I like to keep tabs on as many of my adoptees as I can."

I followed Mr. Hanover inside, where he had a warm fire going. Two black kittens were curled up on a chair next to the fire, sleeping. Mr. Hanover had a tastefully decorated Christmas tree in the corner of the main living area. Both kittens jumped up and ran over to where I sat down on the sofa. I picked up one and Mr. Hanover took the other.

"Can I get you something to drink?" he offered.

"Thanks, but I can't stay long. I just wanted to stop by to check in on the brothers, and to ask you about Holly Jolly, if you have a few minutes."

"I heard about what happened. It's such a shame."

"Mrs. Jolly's neighbor told me that you stopped and chatted with her from time to time."

Mr. Hanover's face softened. "She always saved me some of the cookies she baked. She was at work when I delivered the mail, so we didn't connect all that often, but sometimes she'd leave me a box of her latest creation on the porch, with my name on it."

I could tell that, unlike anyone else I'd spoken to, Mr. Hanover felt genuine affection for the woman.

"I'm putting together a memorial service for her," I explained, then told him about my plan to do something at the service on Sunday and mentioned my interest in learning more about the mysterious woman's life. "I wondered if you had any insight as to why a woman with so much love to give lived her life in such an isolated state."

Mr. Hanover hesitated as he studied me. I realized he *did* know something and was trying to decide whether he should share it with me.

"Anything you feel comfortable sharing would help," I said encouragingly.

"I'm afraid I don't know anything about her that would be appropriate for a funeral service."

I could tell Mr. Hanover knew something he wasn't telling, so I decided to be honest about the rest. "I really am putting together a service, Mr. Hanover, but I'm also trying to figure out who might have killed her. If you have any information at all about her life in Ashton Falls or her life before moving here that might give me some insight into a possible motive, I would be very grateful if you would share it."

"Are you working with Sheriff Salinger again?"

"Indirectly."

Mr. Hanover seemed to be pondering my request. He got up and tossed another log on the fire, then straightened a sofa cushion that someone—probably one of the cats—had disturbed. By the time he sat back down across from me, he seemed to have come to a decision.

"I don't suppose it would hurt to tell you at this point," Mr. Hanover began. "Holly is dead, so they can't hurt her. Not that the people who would want to hurt her have been around for years anyway."

"Hurt her?" I asked. Suddenly Mr. Hanover had my full attention.

He arranged the kitten, who had jumped back onto his lap, as he settled in to tell his story. It looked as if he was taking a moment to gather his thoughts, deciding exactly what he was going to say.

"When Holly was a little girl her father was a money manager who testified against some very powerful people. She never went into specifics, but I got the sense the people he testified against were dangerous. As a result of this testimony, Holly's family lived in hiding. They assumed new names and identities and relocated to an undisclosed location. Ever since she was a little girl Holly had been taught not to talk to people, not to invite them into her life. I guess the people who were after her dad were well connected and out for revenge. Holly said the family had to relocate every few years just to be certain they stayed one step ahead of the people looking for them."

"Wow. I wonder who those people were."

"She never said. I'm not entirely certain she even knew. She was just a child when her life on the run began, and I think living as a chameleon was the only thing she really knew. She told me that it got to the point that she couldn't even remember her own fake name at times."

"Seems like she'd remember Holly Jolly," I said.

Mr. Hanover smiled. "That came later. When Holly was sixteen she did the unthinkable. She fell in love with a boy who attended the same school she did. She knew she wasn't supposed to let anyone in on her background, but it seems she'd begun to share small parts of her past with the boy. When her father found out she'd developed a relationship with the young man he sent her away, and she never saw either of her parents again."

"Sent her away? Sent her away where?" I asked.

"He arranged with a priest to house her in a parochial boarding school until she turned eighteen. It was a week before Christmas when she was removed from her family, and when she was asked her name there, she told the nun on duty she was Holly Jolly. Apparently, it stuck."

"What a sad story. I guess I can see why she learned to avoid intimate relationships. There must have been a part of her that realized that intimacy led to pain and isolation. Why did she tell you this?"

"I caught her in a weak moment maybe ten years ago. I stopped by her house for a cup of coffee on a snowy day, and she'd just found out that her mother had passed away. She was in deep mourning over the fact that she'd never see her again and I was a sympathetic ear she'd grown to trust. I think she always believed in the back of her mind that if she was good and followed the rules, her parents would one day come get her."

My heart bled for the woman. I guess I could understand that her parents had sent her away to protect her, but how awful to be abandoned that way. I couldn't imagine living a life where it was necessary to keep everyone at arm's length.

"Do you know how she found out about her mother?" I asked.

"The priest she had been sent to had received a letter from her mother. Apparently, she had cancer and knew her time on this earth was at an end. She wanted to try to explain to Holly why she and her dad had felt they needed to remove themselves from her life. Holly didn't go into a lot of detail, but she did share that the letter enlightened her as to the fate of both of her parents. She hoped it might bring her peace, but instead it brought her despair. Mrs. Jolly wasn't a drinker—I'm fairly certain she never drank more than a small glass of sherry from time to time—but on the day in question she had a half bottle of brandy on her kitchen counter. I honestly believe that if her inhibitions hadn't been affected by a combination of the brandy and her grief she never would have told me what she did."

"Did she ever bring up her past with you again after that one incident?"

"No. Never. She went back to avoiding all references to her past, and I decided to pretend the conversation had never occurred. I think she was grateful for that. I know the cookie offerings became a weekly thing."

"Poor Mrs. Jolly," I sympathized. "To have been forced to live a life in isolation due to circumstances over which she had no control. Do you have any idea who might have killed her?"

I hadn't planned to ask that particular question, but it seemed Mr. Hanover knew the woman better than anyone.

"I wish I knew."

"Do you think it could have anything to do with her background?"

"I don't see how. Holly never told anyone about her past except me, and I've never told anyone until now. What happened, happened a long time ago. Whoever wanted to hurt her must be long dead by now. I would imagine that by the time Holly moved to Ashton Falls the danger to her had passed. And at any rate, the people were after the father, not the child. I think by that point living with walls she had spent a lifetime building was all she knew."

I decided to stop off at Donovan's after leaving Mr. Hanover's house, to drop off the new piece I'd purchased for Dad's Christmas Village. Like most of the other shops in town, Dad created an elaborate Christmas display in Donovan's window every year. Initially, I figured I'd just deliver the carriage I'd purchased the next time I saw him, but after hearing Mr. Hanover's story I felt I was in need of a parental hug.

"Zoe, how nice to see you," Dad said as I walked through the front door of the store to be greeted by the warmth of the fire, the smell of cinnamon from the candles, and the sound of "Silent Night" playing in the background.

I hugged my dad as I set the box with the carriage on the old wooden counter that was lined, as always, with jars of penny candy.

"I brought you a new piece for your village," I informed him.

"You know, I've been thinking the scene needed a carriage."

Dad opened the box and took out the brightly painted figure. It would go perfectly with the Victorian village he'd created for this year's display.

"I saw it last time I was in New York with Zak and socked it away. I almost forgot to give it to you. I hope you like it."

"It's perfect." Dad hugged me. "Thank you."

Dad walked over to the window and moved a few things around to make room for the newest piece. Last year Dad had done a ski village in the window, and at the time I'd thought it was my favorite, but the tiny English village he had this year reminded me of something you'd see in *A Christmas Carol* or one of those black-and-white Christmas movies.

"So are Scooter and his friend still coming next weekend?" Dad asked.

"As of the last I heard."

"That'll be nice. It's always special to have a child in the house for the holiday."

I looked out the window and watched the snow as it fell gently to the ground. For some reason my talk with Mr. Hanover had me feeling nostalgic.

"Do you remember that Christmas when I was eleven and I was in a major funk and decided I didn't want to receive any presents or participate in the holiday in any way?" I asked.

"Do I!" Dad laughed. "Talk about preteen angst. I was beside myself trying to figure out what to do or say that would coax you out of your bad mood."

I experienced a fresh rush of guilt when I remembered how truly awful I'd been. My bad behavior not only almost ruined my holiday but Dad's as well.

"I remember feeling sad that I was too old for the magic of Christmas and couldn't find a single thing I wanted as a gift. I was past the age for toys but not old enough to really appreciate clothes. I was jealous of my friends who had big families with lots of siblings and moms who baked cookies and made homemade costumes for the school play. I was so horrible to you."

"Any particular reason you're bringing this up now?" Dad asked.

"Actually, I'm not really sure. I just spoke to Mr. Hanover about Mrs. Jolly, and he said some things that made me feel both nostalgic and a bit sad. I'm not sure why that particular Christmas popped into my head. I am sorry, though. You've always been such a great dad to me. I feel so bad that I put you through that."

Dad put his arm around me. "Dealing with difficult stages in your child's life is part of being a parent. I knew you weren't trying to ruin my holiday. You were just confused, and if you remember, what got you upset in the first place was that you got a card from your mom, including a photo of her man of the hour, who happened to have a daughter about your age."

"That's right. I'd forgotten about that."

Dad kissed the top of my head. "And I also seem to remember that we ended up having a pretty fantastic Christmas after all."

We had. Dad had taken me for an overnight stay in the city, where we went to a performance of "The Nutcracker," and then to a really nice restaurant for dinner. An adult restaurant. I remember feeling so special. And he took me shopping in the village and bought me some new clothes, as well as a stuffed doggie that he acknowledged I was probably too old for, telling me to keep it for my own daughter. The truth is, I secretly slept with it for years and still have it. I guess part of me wanted to be an adult and part of me was still clinging to childhood. It was a year of transition, and somehow Dad knew that and found a way to satisfy both the waning child and the emerging young adult.

"I love you." I leaned my head on my dad's shoulder as I watched the miniature train puff its way around the village in the window.

Dad squeezed my shoulder. I wondered if it was a greater act of love to be there for all the moments in your child's life, as my dad has always been, or to send her away in order to ensure that she lived to have one, as Mrs. Jolly's obviously had.

Chapter 5

Although the football team had received their awards at the dinner provided for that specific purpose the previous month, Levi wanted to throw a party for the players and their dates at which they could relax and celebrate the outstanding year they'd had without having to worry about impressing parents or college scouts. I would have volunteered to help Ellie with the food in any event, but the fact that the party gave me the opportunity to mingle with the guys and try to discern what, if anything, they might know about Mrs. Jolly's death was an added bonus.

Levi had provided sodas as well as the ingredients for a festive Christmas punch, while Ellie had baked up a storm to provide a variety of desserts to top off the pizzas Levi had ordered.

"These cookies are excellent. New recipe?" I asked Ellie.

"Actually, they're from a recipe I got from my friend Tracy. I've been trying out different ones for the cookie exchange. So far everything is turning out to be yummy, so I'm having a hard time deciding."

"How's the guest list coming along for the exchange?"

"So far everyone is really excited about the idea. Marijo is bringing those Italian cookies I love and Betty said she'd bring some of her homemade banana bread. My mouth is already watering."

"Mine too," I agreed, then looked around the room. "It looks like pretty much the entire team showed up."

"Levi's pretty popular with the guys, and it helped that girlfriends were invited as well."

The stereo was blasting and a lot of the couples were dancing, while those players without dates were standing around in groups. It seemed obvious by the way Jett and Chelsea were gyrating on the dance floor that they were a couple of the most intimate sort. I must have been wrong about Chelsea having a crush on Levi; it made sense that the head cheerleader and the star football player would be an item.

"I'm going to work the room a bit to see if I can pick up a vibe."

"Vibe?" Ellie asked me.

"Yeah. You know. I'm going to see if someone wants to spill the beans about what might have happened to Mrs. Jolly. I think I'll start with Boomer. I know for certain I saw him in the cabin that day."

"I know we aren't huge Boomer fans, but don't let our dislike of the guy cloud your judgment," Ellie warned. "I saw both Jett and Tyson in the cabin after I arrived."

"Yeah, you're right. Chelsea dropped off some ornaments and Buck dropped off his invoice for the wood. I bet if we really thought about it we'd be able to come up with twenty different people who could have taken the hammer, but Boomer is the only one I know of who had a motive for killing Mrs. Jolly and setting up Levi."

"Why would Boomer want to kill Mrs. Jolly?"

"Because she was going to flunk his little brother, which would have prevented him from graduating on time, which would have delayed him from going to college and possibly making it into the draft and the pros."

"I don't know." Ellie looked doubtful "Seems kind of thin. Boomer is pretty self-involved and doesn't seem the type to go out on a limb for anyone, including his brother."

"At this point thin is all we've got."

I stopped to chat briefly with several students as I made my way across the gym, which had been decorated with red and green streamers. It occurred to me that Boomer, with his shaggy blond hair and letterman's jacket, could have been the student who'd been seen visiting Mrs. Jolly's house a few years back. Of course, there were probably a lot of students with shaggy blond hair and lettermen's jackets who had graduated over the past few years. I knew I was reaching, but sometimes that's all you can do, and hope you come into contact with something.

"Nice party," I said to Boomer, who was chatting with a couple of the football players.

"I figured it was the least I could do. The guys worked hard. They deserved a chance to enjoy their victory."

He figured it was the least *he* could do? I knew for a fact that the party was Levi's idea. What a leech.

"I guess it worked out that no one had to work at the tree lot this afternoon," I commented.

"Yeah, I guess it did," Boomer answered. He crossed his arms, as if to let me know he was bored and I should move on.

"It was a shame about Mrs. Jolly, though," I added.

"Yeah. A shame."

"I heard she helped you out with some tutoring when you were a student," I fished.

Boomer frowned. "Where did you hear that?"

I tried for a look of nonchalance. "I'm not sure. Someone must have mentioned that you used to go to her house for extra help before you graduated. It was really nice of her to go to the trouble. I'm sure her students are going to miss her."

"I guess."

I turned and looked at Jett's friend Tyson, who had been chatting with Boomer but was now standing silently next to me. "Have you decided on a college for next year?"

"Me and Jett have it narrowed down to two. Both are offering us free rides, so we figured we'd visit both campuses before making a commitment."

"It sounds like a good opportunity for the two of you. I hope Jett can get his grades back on track."

"He got that all worked out, so it won't be a problem. I think I'm gonna head out." The boy slapped Boomer on the back.

"Okay. Catch you later," Boomer replied before looking directly at me. "Did you want something?"

"No. Just stopped to say hi. Which I have now done, so I'll be on my way."

Boomer turned and walked away. I rolled my eyes at my lack of interrogation skills. I can't remember the last time I was quite so tongue-tied. I was definitely losing my edge. I'd come to the party to dig for clues, but so far all I'd found out was that Boomer had probably been the student who had been seen at Mrs. Jolly's house and Jett was no longer flunking history.

Across the room, Levi was chatting with a small group of teachers who had dropped by to congratulate the boys. One of them happened to be Lou Barton. I really had no reason to suspect Mr. Barton of killing Mrs. Jolly, but I found I was interested in finding out why he'd been a visitor of the woman over the summer. Not that teachers couldn't be friends and visit each other—but Mrs. Jolly had seemed to adamantly avoid personal relationships of any kind.

"Mr. Barton," I said, greeting him as he conveniently separated from the group on the way to the door.

"If it isn't Zoe Donovan. I thought that was you talking to Boomer. It's been a while."

"Seven years."

"It never ceases to amaze me how time flies."

I couldn't agree more.

"It's a shame about Mrs. Jolly," I commented. "She was always one of my favorite teachers."

Mr. Barton shook his head. "I can't imagine who would want to hurt that woman. We weren't great friends, but we did work together on a project over the summer, and I got to know her a little better. She cared deeply for the kids in her classes."

"You worked together on a project?" I asked.

"You heard she took over as staff adviser for the student paper?" he asked. "I helped her write a grant application we hoped would allow us to upgrade our equipment, including a new printer. She put a lot of hours into it. It's a shame she'll never know that the money came through, as we'd hoped."

"I don't suppose you have any theories as to who might have killed her? Did she have any enemies among the staff members?"

Mr. Barton frowned. "I can't think of a single person who didn't like and respect her. She worked hard and mostly kept to herself. I can't imagine anyone at the school could be guilty of such a thing."

"Probably not, but it never hurts to ask."

"I've heard rumors that you've been sleuthing on the side. Chasing after cold-blooded killers is a dangerous pastime. You be careful now."

"I will, Mr. Barton."

I chatted with the man for a few more minutes before he excused himself and left.

"So has the great Zoe Donovan managed to solve the case?" Ellie walked up beside me after Mr. Barton walked away.

"Not even close. I'm really off my game. Maybe I should just go home."

"Did you forget you're supposed to be helping me with the food and the cleanup?"

"Oh, yeah. I did forget about that in all the striking out."

Ellie laughed. "I might have a clue for you. I was refilling the punch bowl and overheard two of the cheerleaders talking. It seems Chelsea threatened to break up with Jett a few weeks ago if he didn't get his grades back up."

"Chelsea cares about grades? She doesn't seem the type."

"I don't think she cares about grades," Ellie corrected. "I think she cares about dating the big man on campus when the couple goes to college. Based on the conversation I overheard, Chelsea indicated that if Jett didn't get into college she was going to dump him and hook up with Tyson."

"Just like that? What if Tyson wasn't interested?" I asked.

"You've seen the girl. All the guys are interested. Right now Jett is the top dog. If that ceases to be true you'd better believe that Chelsea will move on to whoever takes his place, which at this point is Tyson."

I looked across the room to where Jett and Chelsea were practically *doing it* on the dance floor. "Which gives Jett a really strong reason to want Mrs. Jolly out of the way. She told me that he wasn't all that concerned about not graduating, but I bet he was concerned about losing his girlfriend."

"There's more," Ellie continued. "One of the girls I was eavesdropping on mentioned that Jett wasn't the only Jarratt brother Chelsea has been hooking up with."

I frowned. "Chelsea and Boomer?"

"That's what I heard."

"But Boomer is a coach and Chelsea is a minor," I pointed out.

"Boomer is only a few years older than Chelsea, so unless someone complained I doubt it would be an issue. The thing is that one of the girls in the group said one of the teachers had seen the two of them together. She didn't say which teacher, but if it had been Mrs. Jolly…"

"Then Boomer might have a reason to want her dead as well," I completed Ellie's thought. "I can't see Principal Lamé loving the idea of one of his staff members hooking up with one of his students."

"I figure that if Mr. Jarratt has an extra key to the cabin either son might have access to it. And while we didn't think Jett would set up Levi…"

"Boomer totally would," I concluded.

I looked across the room to where Boomer was chatting with Chelsea's friend Lizzie. If something was going on with Boomer and Chelsea, Lizzie would probably know about it. I wondered if I could get her to talk. Boomer wasn't going to spill the beans; he had the most to lose if his relationship with Chelsea came out. Of course, all we had at that point was hearsay, and it was possible Boomer and Chelsea hadn't hooked up and, girls being girls, some of them were just gossiping to keep life interesting.

"We need to find out if there's any truth to what you overheard," I decided.

"I doubt either Chelsea or Boomer will come right out and admit it, even if it's true."

"Maybe not, but Lizzie might be persuaded."

"You think?" Ellie asked.

"It couldn't hurt to ask. Do we have any ice?"

"There are a couple of bags in the kitchen."

"Dump them."

"What? Why?" Ellie asked.

"Because we're going to make our way over to where Lizzie is talking to Boomer and you're going to ask me to go to the cafeteria for more ice and I'm going to ask Lizzie to come with me."

"Oh. Okay. That's a good plan."

Ellie and I nonchalantly made our way across the room to put our plan into action. I greeted Lizzie just a few seconds before Ellie hurried over and asked me to get the ice. She indicated that she'd need at least two large bags. I asked Lizzie if she would help me and she agreed. Plan developed; plan implemented. Things were looking up.

"I was surprised to see Jett and Chelsea together," I casually commented as I set off across the campus with Lizzie at my side.

"Really? Why? They've been a couple all year."

"I heard Chelsea and Boomer had hooked up. I guess I just assumed Chelsea had broken up with Jett."

Lizzie didn't even look surprised that I knew about Chelsea and Boomer, which I found interesting in and of itself.

"Chelsea likes to play around, but she wants to be a pro football player's wife. Boomer is never going to make the pros now, so she'd never dump Jett for Boomer. Chances are if they were together it was just so she could make Jett jealous enough to handle his grade problem with Mrs. Jolly."

"I guess that won't be an issue any longer," I said.

"Yeah, I guess not." Lizzie sighed. "It's really too bad what happened to Mrs. Jolly. I was totally flunking three of my classes and about to get kicked off the cheerleading squad, but she helped me every day at lunch until I got caught up. She was an awesome teacher. I'm really going to miss her."

It was nice to find a student who actually cared about the woman.

"So why do you think Jett turned down Mrs. Jolly's offer of tutoring?"

Lizzie shrugged. "I guess he figured he'd fix things another way. His dad has a lot of money and there are a lot of important people in the alumni association. I doubt Mrs. Jolly would have actually flunked him. I know she grades fair, but there would have been a lot of pressure to pass him if she'd lived. I hear Lamé fixed all his grades; he's got a solid B average now."

"He can do that?"

"He's the principal. I guess he can do anything he wants to do." Lizzie stopped walking. "Do you have the key?"

"Key?"

"To the cafeteria. It's locked."

Darn. I hadn't considered that. I hoped Ellie hadn't actually tossed the ice, as I'd instructed.

"I didn't think about the key."

"I think I saw a janitors' cart by the boys' bathroom," Lizzie said. "He can let us in."

"So do you plan to go to college?" I asked her as we walked back toward the place she'd seen the cart.

"No. I'm going to get a job here in town. I wanted to go with Chelsea, Jett, and Tyson, but I don't have the grades for a scholarship and my family can't afford to send me to a good college without a scholarship."

"Did Chelsea get one?" I wondered. I knew her family, and they weren't any better off financially than Lizzie's.

"No, but she had the chance to earn some extra money on her own. I think she's going to pay her tuition on the installment plan. Actually, she was kind of vague about the details, but she said she had it handled. Oh, look—there's the janitor talking to Mr. Barton. I'll run and get the key; wait for me here."

It was nice of Lizzie to do the legwork, but waiting made me feel like an old woman. I was twenty-five, not sixty-five, and was about to announce that I'd go with her when I noticed that Boomer and Tyson were talking behind the building that housed the bathrooms. Maybe I'd try a little eavesdropping of my own. I inched as close as I dared and listened.

"It has to be tonight," Tyson insisted.

"I'll try, but it's going to be tough."

"Just do it," Tyson said before walking away.

Do what? I wondered.

Chapter 6

"Do you think we can put on some rock for a while?" Levi asked. "All this Christmas cheer is grating on my nerves."

"Don't be a Grinch. This is a tree lot. A *Christmas* tree lot," I emphasized. "People expect Rudolph and Frosty, not Mick Jagger and ZZ Top."

"Bruce Springsteen has a fun rendition of 'Santa Clause Is Coming to Town,' and Elton John's 'Step into Christmas' is a real toe tapper," Ellie offered. "I bet there are others. Maybe we can mix up the tape a bit."

Levi rolled his eyes and walked away.

"What's his deal?" I asked.

"Seems like Scrooge is alive and well." Ellie sighed. "On a more positive note, the cookies I brought are selling like hot cakes. I think Lamé is going to be very satisfied with the funds we're raising, even though we got a late start. And Zak's Santa thing should be a huge success. By the way, where is Zak?"

"He's not coming until eleven. Scooter arrived last night with his friend and he wanted to let them sleep in."

"That's right. I forgot Scooter was supposed to arrive yesterday. How did it go?" Ellie asked.

"It went great, except that we had to prepare a second guest room when we found out that Scooter's friend Alex is a girl."

"A girl? Really? And Scooter never mentioned it?"

"No, he just said he was bringing his friend Alex and we came to our own conclusions. She's a sweet little thing, not at all like Scooter. Not that Scooter isn't sweet, but he tends to be loud and energetic, whereas Alex is quiet and very mature."

"Wow, Scooter has a girlfriend." Ellie grinned.

"I don't think she's girlfriendish. I think she's just a friend who happens to be a girl. The kids are only nine," I reminded my best friend.

"I seem to remember you and Jerry Connolly telling everyone you were getting married when you were nine," Ellie reminded me. "You even handed out handwritten invitations during recess."

I frowned. "I'd forgotten about that. Now that I think about it, I remember I kissed him and everything. A closed-eye, closed-lip, very quick kiss, but a kiss nonetheless. You don't think Scooter and Alex . . .?"

Ellie shrugged.

"Nah," I decided. "Scooter burped the alphabet at dinner last night. I'm sure if Alex was his girlfriend he'd show more restraint."

"I don't know." Ellie laughed. "Burping the alphabet is considered to be quite a manly act in the eight-to-twelve age range."

"Two hot chocolates, please," an adorable little girl with long brown ringlets and the bluest eyes I'd ever seen requested.

"Don't you look cute?" I commented.

The girl had on a white sweater with a Santa head on the front and green corduroy pants. I had to suppress the urge to embrace this child I'd never met before, which most likely would have scared her, but she looked so huggable.

Huggable? What in the heck was wrong with me? I wasn't at all the type to want to randomly hug cute kids. Maybe I was coming down with something.

"Did you find a good tree?" Ellie asked as she poured the drinks.

"My dad found the best tree. It's tall and skinny and will fit perfectly in our house."

"Wonderful." Ellie handed the girl the cups after accepting the two-dollar donation. "Do you have a small house?"

"We have a big house, but Dad has lots of stuff, so we need a skinny tree. We get to decorate it when we get home. Just the two of us."

"That sounds fun." Ellie handed the girl a couple of napkins.

"Dad even said I could put the star on the top. My mom used to do it, but she died. Her name was Malory, just like mine."

Uh-oh. I noticed the urge to hug on Ellie's face as well.

"Malory is such a pretty name," I said.

"Malory Masterson. My dad calls me his little M&M."

"That's a great nickname," I added.

"Be careful not to spill your chocolate on your cute sweater," Ellie cautioned.

"I'll be careful," she assured Ellie.

"She sure is a cutie," I commented as the girl walked away.

"Yeah. She really is."

There was a wistful look in Ellie's eyes. I knew how much she still wanted children, despite the fact that she seemed to have given up her campaign to have one.

"We're going to decorate our tree later this afternoon if you want to come by and help. You can meet Alex and say hi to Scooter. Zak got a huge tree, so we really could use lots of help."

"Thanks; I might do that. Is it okay to bring Shep?"

"Of course. Plan to stay for dinner. It'll probably be pizza or burgers, but it will be pizza or burgers served with holiday cheer. Oh, look, there's Zak. I guess I'll go help him set up."

As soon as we arrived back home I went up to the attic to find the Montgomery family ornaments my mom had told me about over Thanksgiving, while Zak set up the tree in the stand. As I'd told Ellie, Zak had gotten a large tree. A *very* large tree. To be honest, I was beginning to doubt Zak's ability to get it into the stand. Levi and Ellie both had promised to stop by after they closed up the tree lot for the evening, but at this point it was just Zak and Scooter attending to the chore.

"Wow, look at all this stuff." Alex gasped as she followed me into the dusty room with the A-frame ceiling and large round window that looked out over the lake. "Where did it all come from?"

"Some of it belonged to my family." I explained about Ashton Montgomery, who'd built the town, and Preston Montgomery, who'd built the house. "And some of it was stuff Ashton found in the houses of Devil's Den, the old mining town that used to be in this location. He didn't want to throw away things like photos and journals, so he kept them, and at some point my grandfather ended up with the boxes. My mom told me that they've been up here since the house was built when she was just a little girl."

Alex opened one of the boxes and picked up a photo that was on top. She held it reverently in her hands and said, "It must have been so cool to live back then."

"Oh, I don't know," I argued as I began sorting through the boxes to find the one I was looking for. "I'm pretty attached to indoor plumbing and modern medicine."

"But look at the families. Children, parents, grandparents, all living in the same home. All together for a meal at the end of the day. It must have been wonderful." A dreamy look came over Alex's face.

I stopped to look at her. Other than her appearance, she in no way resembled a nine-year-old girl. She exhibited articulate speech, was extremely smart, and obviously possessed very deep thoughts. It was obvious she was intelligent, very well educated, and had been raised by adults who treated her as an equal rather than a child.

"How long have your parents been gone?" I asked.

"Five months this time."

"This time. Do they go away often?"

Alex shrugged as she dug into the box in search of more photos. "They have to travel for work. I don't mind. It's always been that way, and what they do is really important."

"And when you were younger? Before you were old enough for boarding school?"

"I had nannies to watch out for me. They were nice and I liked them. I didn't miss out."

I just looked at her. She looked back.

"I hear people talking. They say things about my missing out on the things a child should have. But I have stuff. I've traveled all over the world. I get to attend a really good school, I can speak three languages, and I'll easily get into the Ivy League college of my choice."

Ivy League college? I couldn't even spell college when I was nine.

"So what do you like to do for fun?" I asked as I resumed sifting through boxes.

"Fun?"

"Yeah. You know, the stuff you do when you aren't studying, learning languages, or traveling with your parents."

Alex appeared to be thinking about it. "I like to read."

I smiled. "I like to read, too. *Nancy Drew* was my favorite when I was your age, although I read all the *Hardy Boys* as well. What sort of things do you like?"

"I'm reading *A Tale of Two Cities* right now. I like it okay, but I preferred *Emma* by Jane Austen.

Emma had a certain spunk I admire. What are you reading right now?"

"A mystery. A cozy mystery, to be exact. Call me old-fashioned, but I like my murders. What else do you like to do? Besides reading?"

Alex gave this question more thought. "I like to draw. I have a sketchbook. I'll show it to you if you want. I'd like to sketch this room. The round window looking out onto the lake looks like a magical portal to a wonderful fairyland."

I looked at the window. Alex was right. It was exactly the sort of window that could lead to a magical land. "I'd like to see your sketches." I sat back on my heels. "What sort of things do you like to draw?"

"All sorts of things. Things I see. Things I imagine. Sometimes things I dream of and hope for. I drew a sketch of what I imagined you looked like before we came. Scooter told me about you and I knew you'd be both beautiful and friendly. I'm very happy I was right."

"Aw, thank you." I had that sudden urge to hug again. And possibly cry.

"Look at this." Alex held up a small black book with a leather cover that she'd found in the box she was sifting through.

I peered over her shoulder. "It looks like it was written in a foreign language."

"German," Alex confirmed as she thumbed through the pages. "It's a diary written by a woman when she first moved to Devil's Den."

"You can read German?" I asked.

"Yes, as well as Spanish and French. Is it okay if I keep this to read? I'll put it back when I'm done."

"Absolutely. Feel free to read through anything you find."

"All this stuff makes me feel like I've just discovered a wonderful treasure. I can't wait to get started learning about the history of this area. Don't you find it fascinating?"

"Yeah, I guess." To be honest, I hadn't given it that much thought. "There certainly are a lot of boxes up here. I guess it might be fun to go through them sometime. As for the decorations, I suppose we should just bring down what we really want to use rather than carting everything down and then carting everything back up again."

"Is there an angel?" Alex asked. "For the top of the tree? I've never had a Christmas tree of my own, but I always imagined having one with an angel."

I dug through a box I'd already set aside. I was pretty sure I'd seen an angel in it. "You never had a Christmas tree?" I asked.

"My mom doesn't like them. She says they're messy and unnecessary. Besides, we're usually away at Christmas. Last year we were in Africa. It was fun, but I've always wanted to have snow for Christmas. My mom told me we spent Christmas in Aspen when I was a baby, but I don't remember it. I'm pretty sure that until now that was my only white Christmas."

"And now you'll have lots of snow for Christmas," I promised.

Alex smiled. "I will. Do you snowboard? I've always wanted to learn. I saw it on the Olympics and it looked really fun."

Finally: a kid wanting to do something kids should like to do.

"I do snowboard. Would you like to go together this week? I'm sure we can rent you a board just your size."

"Tomorrow?" Alex showed the first sign of real childlike excitement since she'd arrived.

"Tomorrow would be perfect."

After we'd decorated the tree, had dinner, visited with Levi and Ellie for a bit, and gotten the kids to bed, Zak built a fire and poured some wine while I lit a few candles and turned on the stereo to soft Christmas piano. Charlie and Bella were both sound asleep. I imagined they were worn out from playing with Scooter all day. Marlow was lying on the back of the sofa, and I'd seen Spade curled up in Alex's bed. I'm not sure I can accurately describe the look of delight on Alex's face when he joined her as I tucked her into bed. I imagine the girl had never had the opportunity to have a pet of her own.

"The tree looks great." Zak kissed the top of my head as he sat down on the sofa next to me. "It looks so pretty with all the colored lights. Maybe we should leave it up all year."

"Or not." I snuggled into Zak's side. We'd turned out all the lights except the Christmas lights on the tree and mantel. The only other illumination came from the flickering candles and the low-burning fire. "It is romantic, though," I had to admit. "To be honest, I pictured our first Christmas as a committed couple to be quite a bit different."

"Different how?"

"Oh, I don't know. More romance, less chaos."

"Are you unhappy that Scooter and Alex came?" Zak tightened his arm around me.

"Not at all. I have to admit it did give me pause when it occurred to me that candlelight dinners in front of the fire would be replaced with pizza and fart jokes, and long soaks in the hot tub under the stars would give way to kids splashing around in the pool. But I'm really enjoying having the kids here. And Alex is just so great. My heart breaks for her every time I think about the fact that she's so alone in the world. I know I can't replace the mother she longs to be with over the holiday, but I can be one heck of a stand-in big sister. We're going snowboarding tomorrow."

"That's perfect." Zak settled his chin on the top of my head. "Scooter asked me about taking the snowmobiles out."

"Do you think this is what it will be like when we have kids?" I asked. "You'll take the boys fishing and snowmobiling and I'll take the girls shopping and snowboarding."

"Shopping? You hate to shop."

"True. I guess you'll need to take the girls shopping and I'll take the boys camping."

I tried to picture what mini Zaks and Zoes might look like. Would they be tall like Zak or short like me? Would they have Zak's blond hair or my brown?

"I guess we'll have to be sure to have some of each so there are enough kids to go around." Zak ran his finger down my arm.

"Um," I cooed as I felt myself begin to relax after a long day.

"Do you ever think about having kids?" Zak pursued.

Did I? Not really, but there was something about Alex that was bringing out my mothering instincts. I guess it was because she really needed a mom and I felt like she deserved one who would be there for all the special moments in her life.

"I guess I haven't thought about kids all that much," I answered. "I'm still getting used to their being an *us*, so I'm not sure I'm ready for a *we*. But I did have fun today. I think I can understand the bond you feel with Scooter."

"But you want kids?"

"Yeah. I want kids. Someday. We have this big house; it would be a shame not to fill up all those bedrooms."

"There are a lot of bedrooms," Zak cautioned.

"Okay, so maybe we don't need to fill them *all* up. But a couple of kids would be nice. A boy and a girl. I never had siblings growing up and, although I love Harper, I always felt like I missed out on something by not having a sibling closer to my own age. Levi and Ellie were great and filled the gap, but in some ways it isn't the same as having a sister who belongs to you. I used to fantasize about having a sister to share a room with and tell my secrets to. And every little girl yearns for a big brother to watch over and protect her."

"You don't seem the type to let anyone—even a big brother—watch over and protect you," Zak pointed out.

"True. But siblings would have been fun. Levi used to complain about his sister all the time, but I could tell they were close."

"Maybe we'd better have four kids. Two boys and two girls, so the girls can have sisters and the boys can have brothers."

I laughed. "I'm not sure it always works out that neatly, but I imagine I could be persuaded to do four."

Zak leaned over and kissed me. A deep, heartfelt kiss that spoke of entwined lives, growing up, and growing old together. Zak's kisses had always promised pleasure, but this kiss . . . this kiss promised forever.

Chapter 7

I found Alex sitting in the kitchen on Monday morning nibbling on a piece of toast and reading the diary she'd found in the attic. I tossed a log into the brick fireplace that served the kitchen and dining nook to create a feeling of warmth on a cold winter day. "I was thinking of making some pancakes and hot cocoa. Would you like some?"

"Yes, thank you."

"You seem pretty focused on that diary," I observed.

"It's really interesting." Alex looked up from the book and smiled at me. "The diary was written by a girl named Addie Hofmann. She was born in Germany in 1928. She came to the United States in 1943, after her mother met and married a US serviceman. I guess the girl and her mother came by ship, but her mother passed away during the voyage due to complications from what sounds to me like pneumonia."

"The poor thing," I sympathized. "Was the man who her mother married with them?"

"No. He was still serving in the war, but somehow he managed to get the woman he loved and her daughter out of the country. The journal doesn't specify whether this was by legal means or not."

"So what happened after her mother died?" I asked as I whipped the pancake batter.

"Addie was met at the port by a friend of the GI. He'd arranged for his brother Isaiah to transport her and her mother to their new home. So far I haven't found a name for the friend or a last name for Isaiah. Anyway, I think Isaiah was just supposed to take the woman and her child and get them settled somewhere that I imagine was arranged by the GI. When he found that the girl's mother had died and that the girl was all alone, Isaiah decided to bring Addie with him on a journey he'd planned."

"A journey?" I asked.

He was going to head west in search of gold. He ended up with Addie in Devil's Den."

"And she was fifteen?"

"Yes. I prefer jam to syrup."

"Grape, strawberry, or apricot?"

"Apricot, please."

"So what happened after that?" I asked as I poured the batter onto the hot griddle.

"I'm not sure. The penmanship is a little shaky, making my translation slow, but I'm working on it. I hope there are additional journals. This one seems to end once she arrives in Devil's Den. I was going to look around some more after we eat, if that's okay."

"It's absolutely okay. Does the journal go into detail about her journey? Her thoughts? The poor thing must have been scared to death. She arrived alone in a foreign country where she didn't know anyone, and then she was taken to a mining camp by a total stranger. I can't imagine how awful that must have been."

Alex took a bite of her pancakes. "These are really good."

"Thank you," I said as I set a cup of hot cocoa in front of her.

"I think Addie was frightened, but what she left behind sounded much worse," Alex continued. "She writes of her fear and uncertainty, but she also writes of hope for a better life. I think she really liked this Isaiah. It seems like he took good care of her. I really do hope there are more journals. I'd like to see what happened after she started her new life here."

"Let me know what you find. Addie's story is interesting. I'd stay and help you look around for the journals, but I need to check in with Levi and then head over to the Zoo. I thought we could go shopping this afternoon. Maybe we can buy you your own snowboard and a new outfit to wear on the mountain."

"I'd love that." Alex smiled. "I had so much fun yesterday."

"I'll come by and pick you up later. Maybe we can have dinner out. Just the two of us. Just us girls."

Levi seemed to have plenty of help at the tree lot, so I decided to spend the morning at the Zoo. Things were slow there, and I knew Jeremy, Tiffany, Tank, and Gunner had it covered, but I liked spending time at the facility. I'd dedicated my working life to being an advocate for the wild and domestic animals that shared my part of the world, and I find that spending time among them helps me to keep my focus. Every time I walk through the front door I experience a feeling of contentment and homecoming that reaffirms that I'm doing exactly what it is I'm supposed to be doing.

"Close the door," Tiffany screamed as soon as I opened it. I stepped inside and closed it quickly behind me. A small puppy that looked to be a terrier mix was heading for the exit. I reached down and scooped him up just seconds before Tiffany reached us.

"Sorry." Tiffany was breathing heavily. "I took him out of his cage to give him a bath because he stinks to Tuesday and beyond, but he managed to squeeze through the little space between the chain-link fence and the wall in the tub room."

I held the dog up so we were face-to-face and looked him in the eye. "You really do smell bad," I informed him. "If you let Tiffany give you a bath, people will be more apt to want to pet you."

The dog's tongue hung to the side as he panted. He really was cute and didn't seem to be the least bit concerned that he smelled like a stockyard.

"So where exactly did this little guy come from?" I asked.

"A passing motorist brought him in. He said the dog darted out in front of him while he was heading out of town. Luckily, he was able to brake in time. I'm not sure where he came from before that. I'm afraid he might have been dumped. The stretch of road where the driver found him is at least a couple of miles from any houses."

I looked at the dog more closely. He sort of reminded me of Charlie when he was a puppy. Charlie had a lighter color coat and a slightly rounder face, but this dog was close enough that I couldn't help but feel a tug on my heartstrings.

"He looks a little like Charlie," Tiffany said.

"That's exactly what I was thinking," I responded.

"Where is Charlie?" Tiffany asked.

"At home playing with Scooter and Alex. Both he and Bella are in seventh heaven having kids to play with. As for this little guy . . ." I looked him in the eye again. He actually looked like he was smiling. I could see the look of impishness in his little brown eyes and knew he was most likely going to be a handful. "Go ahead and bathe him, and then call Scott to have him come take a look at him." Scott is our local veterinarian. "After that, put a notice in the paper and on the board. Someone might be missing him. We'll give it a week, but if no one claims him, we'll put him up for adoption. He sure is cute. I'm sure we'll have no problem finding him a wonderful home."

"He really is a feisty little guy, and he has this look in his eye that leads me to believe he's thinking about things. If I could have animals in my apartment I'd adopt him in a minute."

"One of the hardest aspects of this job is not adopting every animal that comes through the door. It's amazing I don't have twenty-five dogs and twenty-five cats." I handed the pup back to Tiffany. "Is Jeremy here?"

"He's cleaning the wild animal cages. Do you want me to send him up to see you?"

"When he's done."

Tiffany headed down the hall and I walked into my office, hung my jacket on a peg, and tossed my backpack on the floor behind my desk. It was starting to snow and I found myself imagining snowball fights and building a snowman with the kids. We could build a snow fort and warm up afterward with big cups of hot cocoa.

I have to admit I was starting to feel it: that drive that most of us eventually have to be part of something bigger. Something significant. Something that looked a lot like a family. I couldn't help but remember the snowmen I'd built with Dad, Pappy, and Grandma when I was a kid. Somewhere deep inside I realized I wanted that. The whole package. Diapers, first steps, braces, first dates, and a lifetime of memories to fill my own box in the attic.

But not yet. I still needed time with Zak. I knew that once babies came along, romantic evenings by the fire, trips to tropical locations, and lazy mornings in bed would probably become things of the past.

"What, may I ask, is responsible for that dreamy look on your face?" Jeremy asked as he joined me in the office.

"I was just watching it snow. I went boarding yesterday. It was really awesome, but I found myself thinking that it was time for some fresh powder. I hear they expect two feet up on the mountain."

"You went boarding? I thought Zak said he went snowmobiling. Did you go up to the mountain alone?"

"No." I smiled. "I went with Alex. We had the best time. She'd never been on a hill before, but she was a natural. We were riding the intermediate runs by lunch. I'm taking her shopping today to buy her a snowboard of her own, and a new outfit to wear the next time we go up."

"Seems like you've really taken to that girl."

"She's really sweet. I feel so bad for her, not being with her family at Christmas. Doing things with her like snowboarding and taking her shopping is my way of trying to fill the void. I thought that in addition to picking out a snowboard for her, we could get gifts for the boys and then maybe catch some dinner out. And I want to show her the windows. I think she'll really love all the little villages."

"Uh-oh," Jeremy said. "You have that look."

"What look?" I asked.

"The look that precedes a baby bump."

I turned away from the window and sat down behind my desk.

"Don't be ridiculous. I'm nowhere near ready for a baby bump. I'm not even married yet."

"So have you decided on a date for the big day?" Jeremy asked.

I sighed. "Not yet. Maybe in the summer. Or perhaps the fall. I really don't want to think about it until after the holidays. There's already so much going on with the Hometown Christmas, and now we have the kids visiting, and of course Mrs. Jolly's murder investigation."

"Still not getting anywhere with that?"

"No." I leaned my elbows on the desk. "I did talk to Salinger this morning. I wanted to find out if the lock on the cabin had been changed since the antiques store was there and it hadn't."

"Is that relevant?" Jeremy asked.

"Not really. If the lock had been changed it could narrow things down, but the reality is that there were so many people in and out of the cabin all that day that anyone could have taken Levi's hat and hammer."

"What does Salinger think?"

"He doesn't seem to know what to think. He pretty much admitted he's at a dead end with the investigation."

"Did you ever speak to her neighbors?"

"Yeah, but I didn't learn a lot." I didn't feel it was my place to share Mrs. Jolly's sad history, and I doubted it was relevant anyway. "I did find out she had gifts all wrapped for the kids at the preschool. Maybe I should talk to Tawny. She wasn't at the committee meeting the other day when we were discussing Mrs. Jolly. Maybe she knows something that will point me in a direction."

"How did the memorial service go?" Jeremy asked. "I was going to come, but Morgan is teething and had a restless night, so I let her sleep in."

"It was nice." I shrugged. "A bit impersonal, because I never could manage to dig up any stories or memories, but Dan did a good job making her seem like an important part of the community. There was a full house because Dan added the memorial to the regular Sunday service, so that was nice. I think the people who attended who didn't really know Mrs. Jolly in life got to know her a bit better."

"Has anyone arranged the burial?" Jeremy wondered.

"Salinger hasn't released the body yet, and as far as I know no one is asking about it. Dan told me that he'll make the arrangements if a family member doesn't come forward."

"If you're going over to the preschool will you let Tawny know I plan to bring Morgan by for the Christmas party? She's too young to attend the preschool yet, but she already loves playing with the kids, so we stop by from time to time."

"I wonder if Mom would want to bring Harper."

"I'm pretty sure she mentioned going. In fact, I seem to remember something about a Christmas tree sweater for the occasion."

"A Christmas tree sweater? How cute. I might have to stop by myself."

At times it seemed odd to me that Jeremy and Mom were such good friends. Jeremy was four years younger than me and Mom was . . . well, my mom. But Harper and Morgan had been born within a day of each other, and Mom and Jeremy had bonded over diaper brands and baby formulas. I sometimes felt left out of the inner baby circle, but maybe one day soon . . .

After Jeremy and I finished our conversation I headed over to the preschool. When I walked into the building Tawny Upton owned, I was greeted with a warm, inviting feeling. Hand-painted works of Christmas art covered every wall, there was a tall tree with homemade decorations, and the kids were all gathered in a circle listening to Tawny's assistant read a fun story entitled *The Misfit Elf.* I know if I was a kid this was exactly the kind of place I'd want to spend my days.

"Zoe Donovan—just the person I wanted to see," Tawny greeted me.

"You wanted to see me?"

"Yeah. Didn't you get my message?"

I hadn't, but I also hadn't checked my voice mail yet that day. "No. What did the message say?"

"Now that the public school is closed for three weeks I'm offering a special program for kids in kindergarten through sixth grade. I'd heard that Scooter was visiting and had brought a friend. I wanted to let you know about our program in case you needed day care for the kids, but I also wanted to see if they'd be interested in being in our Christmas play. We're assigning parts and having our first rehearsal this afternoon at two. The play will be held in the community center on December 23. It's a simple story with a lot of songs, so no one has to learn very many lines, but it seemed like something Scooter might enjoy."

"I'll call Zak and have him talk to Scooter about it, and I'll have him ask Alex as well. I was going to take her shopping this afternoon, but I suppose we can go later if she wants to do it."

"Wonderful." Tawny smiled. "So if you haven't come in regard to my message why are you here?"

"Can we talk in your office?" I asked.

"Sure. I was just about to take a coffee break anyway."

Tawny led me to her office, where she poured me a cup of coffee and offered me a sugar cookie shaped like a Christmas tree.

"How can I help you?" she asked.

"I wanted to ask you about Mrs. Jolly. I know she donated Christmas gifts for the kids every year, so I was hoping you might know something about her."

Tawny's smile faded. "Holly was an exceptional woman. She donated quite a bit of her time to the preschool and she always had gifts for every child.

I'm having a hard time understanding why anyone would want to hurt her."

"I know what you mean. I'm afraid I'm fresh out of ideas, and Salinger is at a dead end as well. It will be so unfair if the killer gets away. I'm just asking around, trying to pick up clues, no matter how small. Mrs. Jolly just doesn't seem like the type to make enemies."

Tawny took a bite of her cookie. I could tell she was considering the situation because her brows furrowed as she chewed. Tawny could be silly and flighty at times, but she had a serious side as well. I think it's that combination that makes her both a hit with the kids and a successful businesswoman.

"Holly never really talked about her life outside of what she was doing for us," Tawny shared. "She came in during the summer and school breaks and read to the kids. She really enjoyed story time and would often make up wonderful tales that kept the kids glued to their seats. She never said a word about her life in general. I knew she taught at the high school, but I honestly couldn't tell you where she lived, what her hobbies were, or who she socialized with. I know she liked to bake. She often brought in treats for the staff and kids. Her oatmeal apricot cookies are legendary around here. And she must have had money because the gifts she brought to the kids every Christmas weren't inexpensive trinkets. If I had to guess, I'd say that she had a *lot* of money. One year she donated seven bikes and five computers for some of the older kids who come from limited-income homes."

It made sense that Mrs. Jolly might have money. She had a good job and had lived in the same house for over thirty years. She didn't seem the extravagant sort and I knew she drove a modest car. Still, the money angle wasn't one I'd considered before. I wondered who exactly would inherit her assets now that she had passed.

I realized that the easiest way to get this information was to see if Salinger had looked into it. It was the type of thing law enforcement would most likely do right off the bat. Salinger and I were getting along better than we had in the past, so I felt comfortable sharing information with him as long as he was willing to share it with me.

After I left Tawny, I walked the short distance between the preschool and the sheriff's office. It was a cozy, holiday sort of day, with flurries in the air and the town decorated like a Christmas card. I paused to look in the window at Rosie's on the way. The tiny village in the window was lit up as a small model train made its way around the Dickens-themed scene.

I'd called Zak before I left Tawny's place, and both Scooter and Alex had showed interest in the Christmas play, so my new plan for the afternoon included picking Alex up after rehearsal. Zak planned to spend the afternoon and evening with Scooter, so everyone would have something special to do.

"Salinger in?" I asked the receptionist.

"Go on back. He saw you coming up the walk and told me to just send you in."

I thanked the woman and made my way down the hall. Unlike the rest of the town, the sheriff's office didn't display a single decoration.

"Thanks for seeing me," I began politely. "I'm sure you're busy, so I'll get right to the point. I was just talking with Tawny Upton about the gifts Mrs.

Jolly provided for the kids every Christmas, and it occurred to me that she might have had quite a lot of money. Do you know who'll inherit her estate?"

"I do."

"Do you mind telling me who that person might be?"

"Seems like financial matters might be classified information."

"Classified? Really? I just spoke to you this morning, and you seemed more than eager to share."

"We weren't speaking of private financial matters."

I rolled my eyes. "Are we really going to go through all the motions of this particular dance again? You tell me that you can't share information and perhaps I should butt out and mind my own business. I say I will, but I don't. You demonstrate a certain level of indignation when I don't do as you asked, but then you realize I really can help, so you reluctantly agree to cooperate with me if I tell you what I know."

Salinger smiled. "I don't know. I sort of enjoy the dance. It seems anticlimactic if I just blurt out everything."

I laughed. "Yeah, I guess you're right, but I have plans this afternoon, so can we skip the foreplay and get right down to business?"

"Holly Jolly, whose birth name turned out to be Edwina Harrington, left her entire estate to a man living in a residential care facility in Dublin, Ireland."

I frowned. "Dublin? That must be where she went every July."

"I've confirmed that the man is her father. He's been living in the facility since 1975, when he was shot in the head. He's been little more than a vegetable for the past forty years."

"Nineteen seventy-five. That can't be all that long after he sent her to live with the priest."

"It seems after they sent her away, both of Edwina's parents fled to Ireland, where they had family. As far as I know, Edwina's mother passed a while back."

I remembered Mr. Hanover telling me that the reason Mrs. Jolly confided in him in the first place was because she was upset over the death of her mother ten years ago. The letter must have provided Mrs. Jolly with her father's location.

"Do you think her death could be connected in any way to the events in her past?"

Salinger thought about it. "Not really. As far as I can tell, the men who were after the family disappeared after Mr. Harrington was shot. I don't know why Mrs. Harrington never got back in touch with her daughter. Maybe she wasn't a hundred percent confident that the family was no longer in danger and figured it was better to be safe than sorry. If you want my opinion, I don't think Edwina was in any danger once she was separated from her dad, who was the target all along."

"So do we know if she first made contact after she received the letter from her mother?"

Salinger frowned. "Letter from her mother? I'm afraid I don't know anything about a letter. I learned what I know from some folks who kept an eye on the family until after the dad was shot."

"Mr. Hanover told me Mrs. Jolly received a letter from her mother about ten years ago. Apparently, she wrote it before she died and entrusted it to the priest with whom the family left her when they fled. He was instructed to give it to her after her death, and Mr. Hanover believed it contained the location of Mrs. Jolly's father, among other things. I know Mrs. Jolly went somewhere for four weeks every July. I imagine it could have been to visit her father, but I don't know that for certain."

"I'm not sure it's relevant to the current case, but it couldn't hurt to look into the situation further. I don't know if Mrs. Jolly visited her father, but I do know she'd been paying for his care for the past ten years. I imagine the facility is fairly expensive."

I sighed. "I know it's unlikely that Mrs. Jolly's murder has anything to do with the family's past, but on the other hand, the fact that she lived her whole life in hiding only to be killed by some random person seems unlikely as well."

"I suppose stranger things have occurred, but I'll follow up on what you've told me."

"Go easy on Mr. Hanover if you speak to him. I'm not sure he was really comfortable sharing Mrs. Jolly's secret even though she's dead and so no longer in danger from the events of her past. I think you'll get more from him if you take a soft approach."

"Duly noted."

I got up to leave. "Oh, and get a dang tree. It *is* Christmas."

Chapter 8

If it's a Thursday evening I can usually be found at my book club meeting. Since it's Christmas, we've been reading Christmas-themed books all month. This week is Charles Dickens's classic story of three ghosts and a miserly old man. We've had several new members join the book club in recent months, and while I would never say this aloud, there are two or three of them who could greatly benefit from a visit from the ghosts of Christmas past, present, and future. Not that they're misers; it's more that they tend to have a negative view of the world and seem to find a way to work their rant of the moment into current conversations.

Me, I'm a go-with-the-flow type, with a live-and-let-live, love-and-be-loved philosophy of life. Or at least that's my philosophy theoretically. I guess I do tend to climb up on the soapbox more often than I'd like to admit.

At this moment, however, I was happy and content. Things were fantastic at home, the Zoo was doing well, and I was looking forward to a stimulating discussion of the book I'd read not once but many times in my life. I took an appreciative breath of something that smelled like heaven. It seemed, as usual, Hazel had baked up a storm.

When we first began meeting as a group we used to get together in the library, but at some point the meetings migrated to Hazel's warm and inviting house and had remained there ever since. I have to say I much prefer the new venue. Not only does Hazel have a lovely home but she's a fabulous hostess.

I looked around at the living room, which had been decorated for the holiday. If there is one thing you could say for Hazel it's that she has an elegant sense of style and good taste that allows her to create a warm, inviting setting without giving into the urge to buy every gaudy decoration the holiday store sees fit to sell. Personally, I like gaudy. Mechanical reindeer, colored lights, red bows covering green wreaths; the whole loud and messy array. But I have to admit that Hazel's home, decorated in shades of green and gold, looked simply lovely.

"What is that wonderful smell?" I asked as I poured myself a glass of wine.

"It's a very simple recipe Vivian gave me for maple nut biscuits."

"It smells delicious. I can't wait to try them. Speaking of Vivian, Ellie wanted me to remind you about the cookie exchange."

"I'm looking forward to it. How many women are going to attend?"

"There'll be twelve in all. We're asking everyone to bring six dozen cookies wrapped in twelve packages of six cookies each for the exchange. Ellie is going to make a dessert to eat that evening, and we plan to serve coffee and wine as well."

"I may have to come up with a new recipe to bring. I've been looking for a reason to experiment in the kitchen. I hate to make a lot of food when it's just me doing the eating."

"I'm sure Pappy will help you out with that."

Hazel smiled but didn't say anything. She'd been dating my pappy for a while now, and it seemed to everyone that things might just be getting serious.

"Where *is* Pappy, anyway? I figured he'd be here by now."

"He was here, but I sent him out for some cream for the coffee." A loud ding came from the kitchen. "That will be the biscuits." Hazel hurried away.

I wandered over to the table where Phyllis King was pouring herself a cup of coffee. Phyllis is one of the original members of the book club and Jeremy's landlady. When Morgan was born, she'd offered to rent Jeremy her town house for a ridiculously small amount. I knew Phyllis enjoyed the role of surrogate grandma to the eight-month-old baby and got as much out of the arrangement as Jeremy and Morgan did.

"I wonder if Hazel has cream," Phyllis said as she stirred sugar into her cup.

"Pappy is getting it," I informed her. "I think he'll be back any time."

Phyllis took a sip of the black brew. "So how did the shopping trip go?"

Alex and I had run into her while we were shopping for her snowboard and snow outfit. Phyllis is a retired English teacher who spent her life in academia, much like Alex's parents, and the two had hit it off immediately.

"Excellent. We got Alex a great board and an adorable outfit. We tried it out yesterday morning and had a wonderful time."

"She seems like a nice girl. And so mature. I find it hard to believe she's only nine. She speaks with perfect diction and seems to know almost as much about literature as I do."

"She really likes to read. Whenever we're at the house and I can't find her, I know she's up in the attic reading or going through all the old boxes my grandfather saved. She's not only bright but curious as well. It's such a shame her parents aren't here to appreciate what a great kid they have."

Phyllis frowned. "It is a shame, but I know what the pull of academic notoriety can do to you. I guess my own ambition to be published and find recognition is what prevented me from getting married and having children. I must say that while I don't regret the decisions I made, I do find myself wondering how different my life would have been if I'd made other choices. I'm so enjoying spending time with Morgan Rose. And I'm grateful to Jeremy for letting me play grandma. I find that her presence in my life has filled a void I didn't even know I had."

"I'm sure he's grateful that you allow him to live in your town house for half the rent you could get from someone else."

Phyllis smiled. "Yes, our arrangement does seem to benefit both of us. You know, I have some books I'd like to give to Alex. I think she'll enjoy them, and

I do need to weed through my stacks a bit. Can I bring them by the house tomorrow?"

"Absolutely. Alex and I are going boarding in the morning and she has play rehearsal in the afternoon, but we'll be home around four, or if it's easier for you, we can pick them up when we're out."

"Alex is in a play?" Phyllis asked.

"The Christmas play Tawny is putting on," I confirmed. "Alex ended up with the main role because she was able to memorize the lines a lot faster than any of the other kids. Rehearsal is from two to four, if you want to drop by to watch."

"I'd like that." Phyllis smiled.

"The performance is going to be on the twenty-third in the community center."

"I'll be sure to mark it on my calendar. Oh, look, there's Luke with the cream. The coffee is palatable without it, but I do find it adds something."

I followed Pappy into the kitchen, where he began unpacking the groceries he'd brought. It was such a domestic scene and he seemed to know where everything went, confirming my suspicion that he and Hazel were becoming serious. I was glad Pappy had found someone. Grandma had been gone quite a while and I knew he got lonely at times.

"So how's my girl?" Pappy hugged me and kissed me on the top of my head. The best thing about grandparents is that they can make you feel ten years old again, but in a good way.

"I'm good. How are you?"

"Great. How was the boarding yesterday?"

"Awesome. You need to dust off your skis and come up to the mountain with me. It's been a while since we skied together."

Pappy chuckled. "As good as that sounds, I'm afraid my old bones are no longer up to it. I think I'll leave flying down a mountain with nothing more than a pair of ski overalls to protect me from the cold. Is Alex picking it up okay?"

"She's already shredding down the hill with the best of them." I beamed proudly. "She's really something. She's smart and athletic, as well as polite and caring. We're really having fun together."

Pappy smiled. A knowing kind of smile that said so much more than a regular smile.

"What?" I asked.

"Nothin'." Pappy hugged me again.

"The biscuits are ready to serve. Can you carry them out for me?" Hazel asked Pappy.

"Anything for my lady," he answered graciously.

Pappy left the kitchen with the delicious-looking dessert and I wandered over to the sofa, where Nick Benson was talking football playoffs with Ethan Carlton. If you ask me, neither of the men had a clue about who was really going to win, but I didn't say as much.

"Evenin', Zoe," Nick said. "I wasn't sure you were going to make it tonight."

"Why wouldn't I?"

"Just figured with a new murder investigation to occupy your time you might be tied up."

I sighed and sat down across from the men. "I'm not sure what I've been doing can be referred to as an investigation. So far I'm afraid I haven't nailed down a single solid lead. A lot of wishy-washy, weak leads," I clarified, "but not a single thing that really points me in a direction or narrows things down."

"It does seem like you're a bit off your game," Ethan commented.

"Off my game? I'm not off my game," I defended myself.

Ethan chuckled. "There's the spitfire I know and love. The way you were sighing when you first sat down, I could have sworn you'd already given up."

"I haven't given up," I assured the men. "I'm just having a hard time getting up momentum."

"So what do we know?" Nick asked.

I filled the men in on what I'd figured out to date. I discussed all the angles I'd considered, which admittedly weren't many, and asked for input as to where they might try to look next.

"You said Mrs. Jolly was at the tree lot to take photos?" Ethan asked.

"She was at the lot with her camera earlier in the day and indicated that she planned to return after dark to get some additional shots with the lights. I assume that's why she was at the lot at the time of her murder."

"Did you recover the camera?" Ethan asked.

The camera. Of course. If she was at the lot to take photos she would have had her camera.

"There was no sign of it," I said. "Do you think she was at the lot for some reason other than to take photos?"

"I think a better explanation is that the killer took the camera after Mrs. Jolly was dead," Ethan stated.

"So maybe she got a photo of her killer?" I realized.

"Or maybe she got a photo of something else the killer didn't want her to see," Ethan speculated.

It was like a lightbulb went on in my head. I could actually picture a cartoon with that exact theme. "So maybe Mrs. Jolly wasn't killed because of anything she did; maybe she was killed because of something she saw."

Chapter 9

"Did you lose something?" Ellie asked.

I was standing at the back of the tree lot near where I'd found Mrs. Jolly's body, looking around to see if I could figure out what she might have seen that got her murdered.

"No. I was just trying to get into Mrs. Jolly's head," I replied.

"Come again?"

I shared the discussion I'd had with Nick and Ethan regarding the idea that Mrs. Jolly might have been killed because of what she had seen on the night she came to take the photos.

"I think you could be on to something," Ellie agreed. "I was really struggling to figure out what she might have done that would get her killed. Having the misfortune to simply be in the wrong place at the wrong time makes a lot more sense."

Ellie stood next to me and looked around as well. We were at the rear of the lot, near the staging area where Levi unloaded the trees and then attached the wooden stands. Mostly all that could be seen were the trees. Santa Zak was in the front with honorary elves Scooter and Alex, but I couldn't see them from where I stood. I knew the cabin was off to the left, although again, all I could see were trees.

"Maybe someone was using the cover of the trees to engage in some illegal activity, like dealing drugs," Ellie speculated.

"Maybe, or maybe Mrs. Jolly wasn't standing here when she saw what she saw. She could have even been in the front of the lot, which seems like a better place to take photos. Whoever killed her could have chased her back here, or maybe she realized she was in danger and came back here to hide."

"Or," Ellie added, "maybe she was killed elsewhere and then dumped back here."

I frowned. "It seems like Salinger would have found blood in a second location if that had been the case. I'm going to go out on a limb and say that she was killed in the spot where I found her. I just don't know what she could have seen in a Christmas tree lot that would cause someone to hit her in the head with a hammer."

Ellie walked toward the aisle Levi had left open to get a different angle on things. She looked to her left and then to her right. "It was dark. We left the cabin at about seven and the lights went off at eleven. Didn't Salinger say she was killed around nine?"

"That sounds right."

"So the lights would have been on, and they're pretty bright. If she was on the street side of the lot, cars passing on the highway would have seen her, so the killer must have persuaded her to make her way to the back of the lot. She could have been dragged or coerced—or, as you suggested, chased—in this direction. Again, I have to wonder who would have done such a horrible thing, and why use Levi's hammer and plant his hat?"

"I think finding the link between Levi and Mrs. Jolly is going to be the key," I said.

"I know we've brought up this name before, but what about Jett Jarratt?" Ellie asked. "He's the only one I can think of who might have had a key to the cabin."

I frowned. "Maybe, but I've been hanging around helping out all week and he just seems so nice. Like a big, dumb jock. Not to be stereotypical, but he is big and he is a jock, and I think I understand why he's flunking his classes."

"I guess it could still be him." Ellie didn't sound convinced. "Maybe it was an accident."

"How do you accidentally hit someone in the side of the head with a hammer? Maybe the killer is best friend Tyson," I realized. "Perhaps the boys were here for some reason. Maybe to party in the cabin or whatever. Mrs. Jolly comes along and catches them. Tyson doesn't want to get busted, so he hits her with the hammer."

"I don't know," Ellie commented. "It sounds sort of flimsy. Besides, why would you suspect Tyson and not Jett?"

I thought about Ellie's question as I tried to remember something I knew. "When we were at the high school the other day I overheard Tyson and Boomer arguing. Tyson was very insistent that Boomer do something, and he wanted it done right away. I have no idea what they were talking about,

115

but the tone of Tyson's voice left no doubt that he was in charge of the conversation. Tyson is a big guy who's more calculating than dumb. The boys knew Levi was going to be out for the evening because we talked about our plans in front of them. They also knew he had a refrigerator full of beer. I saw them notice it when they went in for water. Maybe they decided to sneak back after we left to help themselves to a beverage. Mrs. Jolly shows up to take her nighttime photos and catches them. She would probably inform them that she was going to report them to Lamé and possibly even their parents. Tyson realizes that his football scholarship could be at risk if he becomes involved in some sort of disciplinary action, so he picks up the hammer that was sitting right there and hits her with it."

"I thought we decided she was killed where she was found," Ellie pointed out.

"Okay, so they lure her to the back of the lot and kill her with the hammer."

"So why set up Levi?" Ellie asked.

I frowned. "Yeah, that piece really doesn't fit. The guys seem to really like him. I don't see them setting him up for a murder over a couple of beers."

"Still," Ellie added, "I guess it wouldn't hurt to ask Levi if any beer was missing. The rest of the story seems to make sense."

"Do you think he'd even know if beer was missing?" I asked. "He seems sort of out of it lately. I've tried to get him to talk about what's bothering him, but he won't say anything."

Ellie paused. "Part of his bad mood could be because of job stress, but I think the major reason for his crankiness is because of me."

"You? What did you do?"

Ellie looked around. I assumed she wanted to be certain there was no one around to overhear our conversation. "Levi found out about the news I got from my doctor."

"I didn't tell him, I swear," I assured her.

"I believe you. I'm not sure how he found out, but he did. He came to the boathouse after he heard, I guess to offer a sympathetic ear. When he arrived he had on his best friend face, but as we talked and I cried and he comforted me, things changed."

I willed myself to remain quiet and let Ellie finish.

"Long story short, we ended up spending the weekend together."

"You slept together," I clarified.

"We did. More than once. It was the best weekend of my life."

"But . . ." I encouraged.

"But then he made a comment along the lines of us getting together in a more permanent way, now that there were no obstacles to our relationship."

I cringed. I thought I could see where this was going.

"I asked him what he meant by that and he responded that now that I couldn't have children, the fact that he didn't want any was no longer an issue between us. I told him that I never said I didn't want children, only that it looked like I couldn't have any. I informed him that in no way had I decided that I wouldn't try the surgery or even adopt. I got really mad and told him to get out of my house and out of my life."

"Ouch. Was this before or after the auction?"

"Before the auction, but after he broke up with Darla."

"Do you think he broke up with Darla because he wanted to try with you?" I asked.

"I believe so. He seemed really happy until we had this conversation."

"But things between you seem okay?" I asked more than stated.

Ellie shrugged. "Yeah. I felt bad about what I'd said after I cooled off a bit. I went to his place and apologized. I told him that I loved him and needed him in my life, and that I didn't want to destroy our friendship over a misunderstanding. He agreed, and we went back to being friends."

"But you think he's still mad?"

"Hurt," Ellie clarified. "I don't know what to do. I'm hurting, he's hurting, but I don't want to be with a man who never wants children. I also don't want to ruin our friendship, and I know he doesn't either, so we both put on our best friend faces and make the best of things. Most of the time it's okay. I got crazy jealous of Estelle when she was here for the bachelor auction, as you know, and I think he's jealous of Peter, even though he and I are just friends. We haven't talked about it again, but I do know that his odd behavior started after that weekend."

"Why haven't you said anything?" I asked. "I've been racking my brain, trying to figure out what's up with Levi. We've discussed that very subject."

Ellie wiped a tear from her cheek. "I know. I'm sorry. I wasn't trying to keep anything from you. To be honest, I was in denial about the reason for Levi's bad mood. I tried to convince myself it had nothing to do with me. I think I even started to believe it. It was easier to pretend that everything was back to normal. But this week, being in the midst of all the holiday magic and witnessing firsthand Levi's lack of enthusiasm, has caused me to be honest with myself and face up to the reality I have no idea how to deal with."

I wrapped my arms around Ellie. I hated to see my friends unhappy, but I didn't have an answer. I knew if they entered into a relationship without dealing with the children issue, they'd both end up hurting the other and the best friend triad we'd enjoyed would be destroyed forever, and that was something I knew none of us could live with.

"So what do you want for Christmas, little girl?" Santa Zak asked as I climbed onto his lap. The Santa sleigh was closed for the day and Scooter and Alex were both helping Ellie in the snack bar.

I whispered my wish in Santa's ear, which produced a huge grin from the man with the white beard. Reindeer Charlie could see that something fun was going on, so he began to bark and run around in a tight circle.

"Unfortunately, adult wishes will have to wait." I hopped down off Santa's lap. "I told the kids we'd go see the sights in town when you were done here."

Zak stood up and got down out of the sleigh. "I need to change, so give me a few minutes. Also, before I forget, there was a little girl with long ringlets and an adorable smile who told me her name is Malory. She wants a puppy for Christmas and she also told me it's a secret. She's really excited about it, so I thought we should talk to her dad, but I didn't catch a last name."

"It's Masterson," I supplied. "I met her last Saturday and I have the perfect puppy for her if her dad agrees. He's a tiny little thing with an adorable personality who happens to look a lot like Charlie."

"She mentioned how much she loved Charlie and his reindeer antlers, so I'm sure she'd be thrilled with a lookalike puppy."

"I'll look up the dad and see if he's open to the idea. How about I go get the kids while you change? I think it's going to be crowded downtown, so we should probably get started."

Zak headed toward the cabin while I walked toward the snack bar.

"Zoe?"

I turned around to find Kimberly Framer, my high school friend Val's little sister, measuring a tree.

"Kimberly, how are you?" I hugged the girl who'd been four years behind me in school. "How's college life treating you?"

"I'm loving everything about it." Kim beamed. "I love my classes and my roommate and most of all my boyfriend, Skip."

"Boyfriend? Is it serious?"

"Very. We plan to get married right after we graduate."

"Wow, that's so awesome." I hugged her again. "Are you planning to move back to Ashton Falls after you get married?"

"No. Skip's on the college football team and has a real shot at making the draft, so we're keeping our fingers crossed."

"That's fantastic. Good luck to both of you. It seems like Ashton Falls is growing our own crop of football potentials for the first time in history. Just don't let Skip get on a motorcycle. I'd hate for his career to end before it starts, the way Boomer's did."

"Boomer's career was over before he had the accident," Kim informed me.

"It was?"

"Didn't you hear? He was booted off the team for using and selling steroids two months before he tore up his leg. He just uses the accident as an excuse for not playing this year, so most people don't know what really happened."

I had to wonder if Lamé knew about the steroids. Or if Levi did, for that matter. "I hadn't heard," I said.

Kim shrugged. "I guess the school wanted to keep it quiet, and I'm sure Boomer did, too. I only know the truth because Boomer and Skip were friends when they both were on the team together. If Boomer hadn't messed things up, he would have been up for the draft next spring with Skip."

I shook my head. "What a waste. Boomer had real talent. I'd be willing to bet he would have been a contender in the draft even without the artificial help."

"Maybe. Skip made it sound like he'd been using for a while, so who knows how much the steroids helped. I'm afraid the dosing issue has become a real problem for some of the players who can't resist having a bit of an edge. I'm just thankful Skip didn't give in to temptation and join Boomer."

Boomer on steroids. Now that was an interesting bit of information I was certain was going to change things in one way or another.

"Well, good luck with the draft," I offered. "Do you care which team Skip goes to?"

"Not really. We'd like to live on the East Coast, but we'll be thrilled with whatever. If the football thing doesn't pan out for some reason we plan to relocate there anyway, to be near his family. He's really close to them, and he doesn't want to miss watching his nieces and nephews grow up if he can help it."

"That's nice, but I'm sure your mom will miss you."

Kim frowned. "Yeah, she will. I know my mom is happy for me, but she's having a fit that this may be our last Christmas together for a while. She's making sure we follow every tradition we ever had, up to and including finding and decorating the perfect tree."

I looked at the tree Kim had been measuring. It was full and fresh and didn't have any bare spots. It looked to me like she'd found a tree memories could be built around.

"Wow, look at all the lights," Alex trilled as we walked along Main Street an hour later. I'd wanted to ask Levi about the steroids, but he'd been busy and the kids were ready to go, so I decided to call him later.

"And the food," Scooter added as we passed a caramel apple cart.

I smiled at Zak as Alex clung to my hand and Scooter clung to his. The early sunset had created a magical wonderland even though it was only five-thirty. There was something about the hustle and bustle of the crowds milling around on the sidewalk as they looked at the windows, or congregating with neighbors inside the brightly lit shops, that gave the small town where I grew up and lived a festive energy filled with laughter and anticipation.

"Can we get some plum pudding?" Scooter asked as we passed a sign advertising the seasonal dessert.

"After we eat dinner," Zak answered.

"There's a spaghetti feed set up in the community center," I suggested. "It's a fund-raiser for the library, and I think there may be carolers during dinner as well."

"Spaghetti sounds good," Zak said.

"I want to go on a sleigh ride." Alex gasped in awe as we passed the staging area for the attraction. "The trail is lit up with those little white lights. I bet it's like a fairy village when you pass under them."

Zak stopped walking and looked at me. "The sleigh ride ends at seven. Perhaps we should start with that and then get dinner. There's ice skating on the pond until nine, so maybe we can do that after we eat."

"Don't forget the pudding," Scooter reminded us.

"We won't forget the pudding," Zak promised. "Have you ever had plum pudding?"

"No. My favorite dessert is chocolate pudding, but any pudding is good."

"Plum pudding isn't actually pudding," Alex corrected him. "It is good, though. My parents and I spent one Christmas in Edinburgh. It was very beautiful. There was a street fair kind of like this one, only there was a carnival and rides. It was probably my favorite Christmas up until this one, which is my new favorite."

Alex looked up at me and smiled. She looked so cute in the red fuzzy hat and mitten set I'd purchased for her. If I wasn't careful I was going to end up heartbroken when she had to return to school after the holiday. Originally, the kids were supposed to stay for three whole weeks, but Zak had received a call from Scooter's grandparents, telling him that they were missing him over the holiday and asking if he could spend the end of the vacation with them. Zak had contacted Scooter's dad, who said it was fine with him, as well as Alex's mom, who was okay with the change in plans as well. As a result, the kids were leaving on December 26 instead of January 4.

"Oh, look at the little Ferris wheel." Alex ran over to a window that was set up to look like a Christmas carnival. She pressed her face to the window as she viewed the scene. Her warm breath in the cold night began to fog the brightly lit window, but she didn't seem to care.

"Isn't it wonderful?" she murmured.

I stood next to her and considered the cheerful scene. "I like the carousel," I offered.

"With the Christmas horses." Alex breathed in delight. "It would be wonderful to have something like that to cheer me up when I'm feeling sad."

I made a mental note to check to see if I could find a carousel to buy for Alex to take home. I'd already decided on several gifts for each of the kids, but the carousel would be something special for her to remember me by.

"Can we eat?" Scooter chimed in.

"We were going to do the sleigh ride first," I answered.

"But I'm hungry."

I looked at Zak, who shrugged.

"We can get a snack and then head to the sleigh." I turned to look at Alex. "We can come back past the window later if you'd like."

"The line for the sleigh is pretty long. Why don't you and the kids get in line and I'll grab some hot chestnuts to tide us over until dinner?" Zak suggested.

"Okay," I agreed as I grabbed each of the kids by the hand and started toward the long line. It had started to snow lightly—not enough to be a problem but just the touch to add to the Christmas setting.

"Ellie said she might try to catch up with us later," Alex informed me. "She wanted to talk to Levi, but when she was done she said she'd text you to see where we were."

"Did you have fun helping her in the snack bar?" I asked.

Alex nodded. "She's really nice. I love it here so much. This is the best vacation I've ever had."

I smiled.

"I told Ellie we'd been snowboarding this week and she said she wanted to join us when we go again if she has the time," Alex added. "She said the two of you have been boarding together since you were kids."

"We have. Levi too."

"I'd rather go snowmobiling with Zak," Scooter joined in. "Where is he, anyway?"

I looked around but didn't see him, which was odd because he's so tall I can usually pick him out in any crowd. "I'm sure he'll be here in a few minutes."

"There he is." Scooter pointed Zak out, carrying several bags of chestnuts.

"What took you so long?" I asked when the kids were distracted with their snack.

"I ran into Ruthie Elwood."

Ruthie had been the next-door neighbor of Lois Washburn, the crazy cat lady of Ashton Falls, who'd been murdered just before Thanksgiving.

"How is Ruthie?" I wondered.

"She seems fine. She wanted to let me know that she'd heard from the attorney of Lois's sister, the woman who inherited Lois's estate; she's donating the property the senior center was built on to the town for continued use as a senior center."

Lois had been threatening to close down the senior center, much to everyone's dismay.

"That's wonderful. I'm sure all the seniors will be thrilled."

"She also told me that due to the fact that both Lois and Jasper were acting so oddly in the months before the murder, the county has had people out taking soil samples and testing the groundwater."

Jasper Green had been Lois's neighbor on the opposite side.

"And have they found anything?" I asked.

"Maybe. Both Lois and Jasper suffered from migraine headaches. Jasper had gone to an unlicensed practitioner recommended by a friend of his who gave him an herbal tea with directions to drink it when the headaches got bad. Apparently, it did help the headaches, so he gave some to Lois as well. Both Lois and Jasper began drinking the tea every day, which was when the problems began. It turns out the tea contained a substance that can cause a variety of behavioral disorders if ingested often enough so that the substance builds up in the body."

I thought of Jasper. The man had been acting like a total loon the day he kidnapped Levi and me.

"Behavioral disorders such as aggression and paranoia?"

"Among other things," Zak confirmed. "Based on what Ruthie told me, it seems the tea might be responsible not only for Jasper's odd behavior but Lois's over-the-top obsession with the cats."

"Wow; that tea sounds like dangerous stuff. Do they know where Jasper got it?"

"Ruthie didn't know for sure, but she thought it was from some little town south of the border. Jasper seems to be doing better now that he's off the tea, so maybe he'll be able to tell the authorities at some point. If the tea did come from Mexico there isn't a lot that can be done, but Ruthie was happy to find out it wasn't the water that was contaminated. She'd been drinking nothing but bottled water for weeks."

"We're next," Alex interrupted our conversation with an enthusiastic squeal.

"It looks like we might even get into the front row," I said.

"I'm going to lean my head back and look up at the lights when we pass beneath them," Alex announced.

I have to admit that sharing Hometown Christmas with the kids was making the event a lot more fun than it would otherwise have been. Not that it isn't always awesome, but there's something wonderful about seeing the magic of the season through the eyes of children.

Chapter 10

"Good morning, everyone," I greeted Zak, Alex, and Scooter, who were all sitting at the kitchen table. Zak and Scooter were eating omelets and talking, while Alex was reading the second diary in the series of three that she'd found.

"You aren't going to eat your eggs?" I asked the girl, who seemed to have tuned everyone out. "Alex?" I asked again when she didn't answer.

"She's been like that all morning," Scooter reported.

I sat down next to her and put my hand on her shoulder. "I take it you found some pretty riveting stuff?"

Alex looked at me with concern evident on her face. "Isaiah had an accident. He's in bad shape and Addie doesn't think he's going to make it."

I frowned. "How far are you into the diary?"

"It's 1945. The mines are drying up and the men who work them have been taking bigger risks to get whatever they can before the gold is gone completely. Addie just had her seventeenth birthday. She's engaged to a man named Tiger Littleman, so I guess she'll be okay if Isaiah doesn't make it, but of course she's extremely distraught because she's grown to love him very much."

"So the man who sent her to the States never came for her?" I asked.

"He was killed in the war. She's remained in Isaiah's care. The doctor is trying to save him as she's writing this passage, but it isn't looking good."

I frowned. The name Tiger Littleman sounded familiar, but I couldn't quite place it. I knew there were artifacts from Devil's Den in the Ashton Falls Museum as well as the library. The museum was closed for the season, but maybe I'd ask Hazel about him when I saw her next.

Alex continued to read. She gasped, and then a single tear slid down her cheek. "Isaiah died."

I put my arm around Alex's shoulder. "Maybe you should put the diary away for a while."

"But I can't. I have to find out what happens next."

"Okay," I agreed, "but first eat your breakfast and get dressed."

Alex set the journal aside and began eating, as I'd asked. It was obvious she felt deeply for the people in the journal, and I could understand her need to finish the story. The fact that she'd done as I asked rather than arguing or complaining was further proof that she was an extraordinary child who had been raised to follow directions and respect her elders. Her parents really were missing out, no matter what anyone said to the contrary.

"What are you boys up to this morning?" I asked.

"Video games," they both answered in unison.

What is it about boys and their games?

"And after that?" I asked.

"More video games," they both shouted.

Scooter started laughing and milk squirted out of his nose, which, I realized, was a *very* nine-year-old thing to do.

"I found a wonderful home for our little scamp," I informed Tiffany when I arrived at the Zoo later that morning.

"Really? That's great. Where?" Tiffany had on a festive red sweatshirt with the Zoe's Zoo logo on the front. It was hard to wrap my head around the fact that it was only three days until Christmas. I was looking forward to it with mixed emotions. On one hand, I couldn't wait for the kids to open the gifts I'd gotten them, but on the other, I was going to miss them when they left.

"I met a little girl named Malory Masterson who asked Santa Zak for a puppy for Christmas," I informed Tiffany. "I spoke to her father, and he's willing to adopt the pup. He'll be by on Christmas Eve to pick him up. I told him that we'd only be here in the morning, but he has a neighbor who'll keep him until after Malory goes to bed."

"I know Malory." Tiffany smiled. "She goes to the same church I do. She's such a sweetie, and she's been through a tough time since her mom died. Her dad works a lot, so most of the time it's just her and the babysitter. A puppy will be good company for her. I wish I could be there to see the huge smile on her face when she sees what Santa brought."

"Yeah, I bet she's going to be so excited, and I'm glad we found the little guy a special home. He's been very effective at worming his way into my heart."

"Mine too," Tiffany agreed. "I really need to find a place to live that will allow me to have pets."

"I'll keep an eye out and let you know if I hear of anything," I promised.

"By the way, Sheriff Salinger stopped by about a half hour ago," Tiffany informed me. "He was in the area and thought you'd be here. He wants you to stop by his office when you get a chance."

"I'll head over as soon as I check my messages."

"There isn't a problem, is there?"

"No. I had some information I wanted to share with him about Mrs. Jolly's murder. He wasn't in this weekend and I didn't want to leave it with the sub, so I just left a message that we needed to talk."

"So how is the investigation going?" Tiffany wondered.

"Honestly, it's been frustrating. I don't want to say too much at this point, but I might have a few leads for Salinger to follow up on. The thing is, I'm not sure they'll pan out. I hoped this would be all wrapped up before Christmas, but it isn't looking that way."

"I guess these things take time. By the way, the lady who adopted the white Persian came by this morning. She's thrilled it worked out for her to take the cat and he seemed to really take to her as well. I was happy he found a home in time for Christmas. It was sad to think of him spending the holiday without a family."

"I like to get all the domestics adopted out for the holiday if possible."

"We only have two more cats to find homes for and then, with the exception of the bear cubs, who are napping peacefully, we'll have an empty house," Tiffany said.

"Wonderful. Go through the files to see if we can't dig up some prospects for the cats. The cubs should be well into hibernation, so if we can get the cats placed we can all have some extra time off for the holiday. If we can't, I'll just bring them home with me."

I checked my messages and returned a few phone calls, then headed back out to have a chat with Salinger. I'd managed to ask Levi about Boomer, and he'd told me he'd had no idea Boomer had been kicked off the college team for using and selling steroids. He wasn't happy about the situation either. I cautioned him to talk to Lamé before he got too upset; the information I'd received had come from a third party and could very well be incorrect. Lamé was off work for the holiday break like everyone else at the high school, but Levi was upset enough that I wouldn't be surprised if he decided to call the man at home.

I was just pulling into the parking lot near the sheriff's office when my phone rang. It was Levi.

"Hey, Levi. What's up?"

"I spoke to Lamé."

"And . . . ?"

"And he assured me that Boomer left the college football team due to an injury, just as we've all been told. I'm pretty sure he was lying. He sounded nervous and couldn't wait to get off the phone. If you ask me, the guy is in on the cover-up. The thing I don't get is why?"

"We know Lamé is all about the money and Boomer's dad has plenty," I reminded him.

"Yeah, I guess." Levi sighed. "I've been thinking about it ever since you told me what Kim said and I've decided I really need to get to the bottom of this. If Boomer is selling steroids, I don't want him anywhere near the boys."

I looked out the windshield at Salinger's front door. "I'm at the sheriff's office right now. I'll ask Salinger to see if he can get the scoop from the college, but they're out on break, too, so it might have to wait until after the first of the year."

I heard someone speak to Levi in the background. "I have to go," he said when he came back on the line. "Someone wants to buy a tree. Call me after you talk to Salinger."

"Yeah, I will." I hung up, pulled my down jacket tight around my neck, and got out of the truck. I didn't have Charlie with me today; he'd seemed to prefer to stay home and hang out with the kids, and I have to admit I was feeling just a tiny bit jealous. Wasn't it the dog who was supposed to be jealous of the new baby and not the other way around?

Salinger was with a suspect involved in a robbery when I arrived, so I was offered the choice of waiting or returning later. I chose the latter. There was no way I wanted to hang out in the sheriff's waiting room all morning. Because I was already in town I decided to head over to Ellie's Beach Hut to enjoy a cup of her excellent coffee. The lakefront restaurant was packed with holiday shoppers, but she managed to snag me a table near the window. Once I was settled she asked her assistant to cover the counter while she took a break so she could visit with me.

The interior of the rustic café was warm and cozy as a real wood fire crackled away in the fireplace and snow fell outside the large picture windows. The lake was pretty much completely socked in with low-lying clouds, which gave the café and the pier it was built on the feeling of isolation, as if we were on an island in the middle of nowhere.

"It's busy," I stated the obvious as Ellie joined me with her own cup of coffee and a plate of pastries.

"Holiday crowd is in town. It's nice you stopped by. My back is killing me, so it's convenient to have a reason to take a break."

"Something wrong with your back?" I asked.

"No, not really. I've just been working hard all week between putting in time here and at the tree lot. I guess I'm just tired. So what are you up to?"

I explained about the delay in my meeting with Salinger.

"Have you talked to Levi?" Ellie asked. "He was really upset about the Boomer thing."

"Briefly."

"He's concerned that Boomer has been giving steroids to Jett and some of the other guys," Ellie said.

"You realize if he goes all Rambo and then it turns out that Boomer is innocent, it isn't going to go well for Levi."

"That's what I tried to tell him, but he wouldn't listen to me. Maybe Salinger can find out why Boomer really left the team. He's a cop; it seems like he'd have access to those kinds of files," Ellie said.

"If we're going with the idea that Mrs. Jolly was killed because of something she saw, what if she went back to the tree lot to take pictures of the lights and she happened to snap a photo that had Boomer in the background distributing steroids to some of the team members? That might be something that would get her killed."

Ellie frowned. "Yeah, but why do the deal there? That doesn't make sense."

"What if the drugs were in the cabin?" I speculated. "It's owned by Boomer's dad, and it's been empty since the end of the summer. It might make a good place to hide illegal drugs and meet customers. Originally, the cabin wasn't going to be used for the tree lot. It was a last-minute substitution and Levi moved in with very little notice. What if Boomer didn't have time to get the drugs out and needed to go back to get them?"

"That actually makes sense," Ellie realized. "So what now?"

"We tell Salinger and let him do the messy part. It's almost Christmas, and I really don't want to end up almost dead or worse again."

Later that evening I sat in the living room with Zak, Levi, and Ellie. The kids were in the den watching a movie, which gave us the ability to speak freely.

"According to Salinger," I began, "Boomer was kicked off the football team for using steroids. The college was unable to prove he was dealing, so he struck a deal to leave the campus in exchange for silence on the part of the university, which was just as happy not to have a scandal to deal with. The motorcycle accident was a convenient coincidence because it gave him a plausible reason to have left the team. No one stopped to question his explanation or dig deeper."

"And has he been selling my boys steroids?" Levi asked.

"I don't know," I admitted. "Salinger interviewed Boomer, who swears he hasn't used since he left the team and never had been a dealer. Salinger seems to think he's lying and is going to keep digging. He wants to talk to the boys, but he needs parental consent."

"And Lamé?" Zak asked. "Did he know the truth this whole time?"

"Salinger spoke to him as well and he says no," I answered. "Again, I believe we should take his assurance with a grain of salt. The problem is that we have no proof to the contrary at this point, so unless new information becomes available all we can do is act as if he's innocent."

Levi put his head back onto the sofa and looked up at the ceiling, then covered his face with his hands. I could see he was frustrated. We all were. At the very least, Boomer had lied and would be removed from his position as assistant coach. The problem was that there might be a whole lot more going on that we had no way to prove.

"What about Mrs. Jolly's murder?" Ellie asked.

"Boomer swears he knows nothing about it and was nowhere near the tree lot at the time of her death," I informed the group. "He told Salinger he was alone at home, watching a movie on HBO, which, unfortunately, can neither be proven nor disproven."

"There has to be a way to link Boomer to the cabin that night," Levi insisted. "He has to be the killer. For the first time since Mrs. Jolly died we have a theory that makes sense. If he did go back for the drugs and she saw him, he would have killed her. That's just the kind of guy he is."

"Yeah," Ellie agreed, "and it makes sense that Boomer would have set Levi up to take the fall. He's been lusting after his job since he returned to town."

I watched Zak as he got up and tossed another log on the fire. He hadn't said much since we began the discussion, which led me to believe he had been thinking things through. He was really great that way. He had a unique ability to control his emotions and look logically at a problem. I'm sure that's part of why he's so good at what he does.

"There are a couple of different things going on here," Zak said when he returned to the sofa. "The first is the issue surrounding the steroids and the question of whether or not Boomer has been giving them to any of the boys on Levi's team."

"God, I hope not. Their college careers will be over before they even begin." Levi groaned.

"I hate to say it, but if Boomer has access to steroids it makes sense that he might be giving them to Jett," I offered. "I don't want to think that's true, but Jett has had a fantastic couple of years."

"If Boomer has been dealing the drugs, then the second issue becomes whether or not Lamé is aware of the activity," Zak added.

"Surely he wouldn't turn a blind eye," Ellie said.

"He wants to win," Levi pointed out.

"He was in the cabin," I blurted out. "On the day Mrs. Jolly was killed. I went inside to find a phone book and ran into him. Literally. He was just standing in the middle of the room, looking around. He said he was there to meet Boomer and he did, in fact, talk to him, but Lamé was acting all fidgety and nervous."

"So maybe we were right that the drugs were in the cabin," Ellie said. "Maybe he was there to retrieve them. He might have arranged with Boomer to move or even destroy them if he realized the cat was close to being out of the bag."

"But I refused to leave, so Lamé did," I informed everyone. "Maybe he came back that night and killed Mrs. Jolly."

"Which we would need to prove," Levi said.

"So to summarize," Zak began, "we have four unanswered questions. We need to find out if Boomer has been dealing steroids. If he has, we need to find out which boys have been using. We also need to find out if Lamé knew what was going on. And finally, we still need to prove who killed Mrs. Jolly."

Marlow jumped up on the sofa and tried to push Charlie's head out of my lap. Spade had been glued to Alex ever since she'd arrived, and Bella seemed to enjoy the more energetic Scooter, but by the end of the day Charlie was exhausted and more than happy to curl up with me, which left Marlow to compete for my attention.

"So where do we even start?" Ellie asked.

"I'm going to suggest we all get a good night's sleep and then check in with Salinger tomorrow," Zak answered. "He might have some or all of the answers by then, and if he doesn't we can come up with a game plan at that point."

Everyone agreed that Zak's idea was a good one and shortly after the conversation wrapped up both

Levi and Ellie left. I decided it was time for the children in the house to go to bed, so I headed upstairs to nudge them toward the getting-jammies-on and washing-up phase of the evening.

"Where's Alex?" I asked Scooter, who was still watching the movie.

"Upstairs in the attic again. She sure does like it up there."

"Yeah, she does. I'll go get her. I need you to get ready for bed the moment the movie is over."

"Okay."

Boy, had things changed. The first time Zak had tried to get Scooter ready for bed he'd destroyed the house, and less than nine months later he was willing to do what was asked of him in a polite and agreeable manner. I guess a little personal attention by someone who cares really does go a long way.

Chapter 11

Sometime during the long sleepless hours I'd spent tossing and turning, I made up my mind that I was going to find answers for Zak's four questions by the end of the next day. An ambitious goal? Maybe. But tomorrow would be Christmas Eve, and if there was one thing I knew it was that I wanted to spend a relaxing day with my friends and family without murder investigations and steroid controversies hanging over me.

I decided that the best place to start my campaign was at the location of the murder. If Boomer had hidden drugs in the cabin it was likely he'd moved them by now, but that didn't mean he hadn't been careless and left clues behind for me to find.

By the time I arrived at the tree lot Levi was busy with customers. Personally, leaving the purchase of a tree until December 23 seemed kind of pointless. It was a lot of work to decorate a tree, and going to all that effort just to take it down in a few days' time seemed, to my mind, like a total waste of time.

I stood in the middle of the main room of the cabin, where I'd seen Lamé standing on the day of Mrs. Jolly's murder, looking around the room for a probable hiding place. The cabin didn't contain much furniture, so hiding the drugs in a dresser drawer or behind a sofa cushion was out of the question. Levi had brought a portable bed for his use and the kitchen remained intact with cabinets, a refrigerator, and a sink, but no oven or stove of any type. I looked through the cabinets, not really expecting to find anything. Which I didn't. The floors were hardwood, and I didn't see any evidence of a trap door. The windows were covered with blinds but no curtains, and there were ceiling lights but no lamps. The one bedroom contained only the bed Levi had brought in and his opened suitcase with clothes spilling out of it.

There were no potted plants or pictures on the walls to act as hiding places. If Boomer had hidden drugs in the cabin, the only possible location might be a hidden compartment within the walls. The problem was that all the walls were covered with hardwood paneling. Finding the hidden compartment, if there even was one, wasn't going to be an easy undertaking.

"Whatcha doing?" Ellie asked when she walked in while I was running my hands over the walls.

"Looking for a hiding place."

"You think Boomer hid the drugs in the wall?"

"It's the only place that makes sense, if he even used the cabin, as we suspect. I realize the drugs most likely have been moved by now, but I hoped if we could find a loose board we could find some kind of a clue."

Ellie began running her hands up and down the wall opposite the one I was working on. "I found out something you might be interested in."

"Oh, and what's that?"

"The cable was out at the time Mrs. Jolly died. I know that because I set up my DVR to record a Christmas movie on the Hallmark Channel that night. When I got home last night I was feeling wound up, so I decided to watch it. When I found out it didn't record I called the cable company, and they verified that the cable went out at seven and didn't come back on until after midnight."

"I'm sorry?" The cable went out in our town fairly often, so I failed to see why Ellie thought I'd be interested in this particular piece of information.

"Don't you see? Boomer told Salinger he was home watching a movie on HBO when Mrs. Jolly was killed. If the cable was out he couldn't have been watching HBO."

"Maybe he has satellite," I suggested.

"I thought of that, so I drove by his house, and he doesn't have a dish. I suppose it's possible he watched the movie on his computer, but it seems like a long shot."

"Hey, I think I found something," I said.

"A loose board?" Ellie asked.

"Yeah, but we'll need something to pry it open the rest of the way."

I looked around the room. There weren't any tools to speak of, but there was a knife that looked as if it had been used to butter toast. I handed it to Ellie, who worked the board until she could pull it away from the wall far enough to slip a hand inside and pull. Behind the board was a box between the studs. Ellie pulled out the box and handed it to me. It was empty, as I expected. I wasn't sure that finding an empty box in a wall was going to help us at all, but maybe it had fingerprints on it, or drug residue or something. It certainly couldn't hurt to give it to Salinger, who I planned to drop in on later that morning anyway.

I was about to replace the board so that it wouldn't be obvious we'd been snooping around when I noticed something farther down in the wall. It looked like a piece of paper. I couldn't reach it, so Ellie went out to the tool shed to see if there was something we could use to fish it out. The sound of "We Wish You a Merry Christmas" playing in the background as I tore apart the cabin in an effort to find a clue that would point us in the direction of a killer seemed paradoxical at best. I could hear the sound of children's laughter and knew that to many of those just beyond the cabin wall, Santa's magical sleigh ride was the most important thing on their minds.

I heard the door open and turned to find Chelsea staring at me. "What are you doing?" she asked me.

"Nothing." I hoped I didn't appear as startled as Lamé had when I'd caught him snooping that day. "I was just waiting for Ellie so we could finish the shopping list I was making. It looks like the snack bar was a lot more popular than we anticipated."

Chelsea frowned. I could tell by the look on her face that she wasn't buying my story. I was standing in front of the hole in the wall, which I hoped she wouldn't notice. I didn't want her tipping Boomer off before we had a chance to prove what he'd been doing.

"Did you need something?" I asked.

"Coach Denton wanted me to find a screwdriver."

"I think all the tools are in the shed."

Chelsea shrugged. "Yeah, you're probably right. If you're going to the store can you get some more diet soda? The guys drank it when we ran out of regular yesterday."

"Yeah, no problem. Any particular flavor?"

"Cola is fine."

Ellie walked in with a long screwdriver just as Chelsea was turning to leave.

"Hey, thanks," she said, taking the tool from Ellie. "Coach was looking for this."

Ellie shrugged at me as Chelsea walked away. "Well, I *had* something we could use to get the paper out of the wall."

I looked around the room. "It's too bad I didn't bring my truck. There are all kinds of things in there we could use. Hand me that long spoon we've been using for the hot cocoa. If I get my arm in far enough that could work."

It took a little finagling, but I managed to work the paper out of the wall. It was a handwritten note with a bunch of numbers that appeared to be some sort of code. If I had to guess, it could very well be Boomer's client list. I stuck the note in my pocket and then headed out to see Salinger and buy the soda I'd promised Chelsea while Ellie opened the snack bar.

I had to smile when I walked into Salinger's office. There was a small decorated tree in the corner of the room. I don't *know* if the tree was the result of my comment the other day, but I'd like to think it was. As you know, my relationship with the man began on a *very* rocky note, but I've convinced myself the man is actually beginning to like me.

I decided not to mention the tree. If I know Salinger—and I think I do—mentioning the fact that he obviously took my comment to heart would only make him growl like a grouchy old bear.

"I found this in the cabin." I handed the box to Salinger. "It's empty, but I figured you might be able to do something with it."

"I see you aren't wearing gloves," Salinger pointed out.

The man had me. I suppose I should have known to wear gloves when handling potential evidence.

"So were you able to get any of the boys to agree to steroid testing?" I knew Salinger had planned to speak to several of the football players parents' to get permission to have their children tested.

"Actually, I did. So far we've only found one boy who's tested positive: Jett Jarratt."

"I'm not really surprised," I commented as I settled into the chair across from Salinger's desk.

"The thing is," Salinger continued, "Jett swore he hadn't been taking steroids or any other drug. He seemed adamant and I have to admit I believe him."

I frowned. "How can that be?"

"It's possible someone is dosing him without his permission. Probably adding the drugs to his food."

"Boomer," I speculated.

"Maybe," Salinger agreed, "although I don't see why Boomer would be dosing his own brother. It would seem he more than anyone would know the consequences of testing positive for drugs."

"But high school students usually aren't tested, so maybe he figured he wouldn't get caught. He probably figured if he discontinued the dosing in time for the drugs to work their way out of his system before college testing, Jett could get the advantage he needed to get a scholarship and no one would be the wiser."

"Maybe. At one point I considered Jett's dad as the doser. He has a lot to gain financially if Jett gets a free ride to college, but he seemed as surprised as anyone when the results came back positive, and he didn't have to agree to the testing in the first place."

"And Tyson?" I asked. He seemed to be almost as good a player as Jett.

"He was clean."

I sat back and pondered the implications of this bit of news. It seemed to me that all roads led to Boomer. Now I just needed to prove it.

After speaking to Salinger I decided to stop by to talk to Hazel about Addie and Tiger. I knew I'd heard the name Tiger Littleman somewhere. Maybe he'd done something important that landed him in the Ashton Falls history books, and if he did, chances were Hazel would know it. She was an expert librarian who seemed to know a lot about a lot of different things.

"Merry Christmas," I greeted Hazel. The library was tastefully decorated for the holiday, and adults and children alike were browsing the aisles and sitting in the chairs provided for sampling books while enjoying the warm interior.

"Merry Christmas to you, too, dear." Hazel hugged me. "I didn't expect to see you in here today.

I'm looking forward to dinner at your house tomorrow."

"And I'm looking forward to having you. Don't worry; Zak and Ellie are handling most of the cooking. Zak mentioned you're bringing a special dish as well."

"Oyster dressing," Hazel confirmed. "I spoke to your mother and she told me that she was going to bring a festive Christmas salad. I know Luke is hoping for some of Levi's hard cider."

After taking into account the fact that we planned to have company on Christmas Eve but would most likely go to my parents' on Christmas Day, Zak had decided to do a big Christmas dinner, with a goose and everything.

"I'm pretty sure he said he'd bring some. The reason I'm here is because I wanted to ask if the names Addie Hofmann and Tiger Littleman meant anything to you."

"Sure. Tiger and Addie were the parents of Hancock Littleman, who helped fund the Ashton Falls hospital."

"Why did he do that?"

"It seems he made a lot of money as a young man and wanted to do something in memory of his parents. He also built the gazebo in the park and dedicated it to all the men and women who lived in the area when it was known as Devil's Den. There's a plaque inside the gazebo that lists, among others, the names of his parents."

"So Tiger and Addie got married and had children."

"Seven of them," Hazel confirmed. "The couple moved from the area in 1949. Why do you ask?"

I explained about the diary Alex had found in the attic.

"You have Addie Littleman's diary?" Hazel beamed. "I'd love to read it."

"I'd be happy to lend it to you as soon as Alex is finished with it. Are you coming to the kids' play this evening?"

"I wouldn't miss it."

As I should have expected, Alex was in the attic reading when I got home. She was sitting in a corner under the large round window, which was cracked open to allow just a few flurries of snow inside. She was so intent on the book she was reading she didn't appear to even realize that her dark hair was flecked with tiny white snowflakes.

"Addie found the key," she informed me as soon as I walked in.

"Key? What key?"

"The key to her heart. Although Addie was engaged to Tiger before Isaiah's death, she couldn't let herself really love him. Not the way a wife should love a husband. She'd experienced so much pain and loss in her life that she guarded her heart and locked it away. Isaiah knew that. He wanted her to be happy. To experience real love. I guess before he died he left her a note, which he entrusted with a nurse. She didn't go into a lot of detail about what was in the note, but she did say that after reading it she did a lot of thinking and finally figured out what Isaiah had been trying to tell her."

"That's so romantic." I smiled.

"I know," Alex breathed. "Addie was an exceptional woman, and she really loved Devil's Den.

It broke her heart to leave. She worried that there would be no one to tend to Isaiah's grave once the town was deserted."

"I wonder if he's buried up in the old cemetery."

"The journal doesn't specify a location," Alex said. "I guess you can go to look in the spring, after the snow melts."

"Not all the graves have markers," I told the girl.

"Isaiah's would. Addie loved him very much. It tore at her heart that he might not be remembered. She was very sad when she moved from the area with her family when the mines closed down. I'm not sure why she left the journals behind. Maybe she figured they were part of her past and she was heading into a new future, or maybe she hoped that someone would find them and read them." Alex looked at me. "Did you know that Ashton Montgomery came to Devil's Den before he built Ashton Falls?"

I frowned. "He did?"

"Yes; he's first mentioned in Addie's journal in 1947. The passage says:

> *"'Now that the gold has run dry, many families have begun to leave. Tiger loves the area and wants to stay, but Mr. Montgomery had been very persuasive in getting the others to accept his offer. I don't know if Tiger will give in to the man, but times are hard, and it's more and more difficult to provide for our basic needs.'"*

"It was my understanding that the town was completely deserted when Ashton bought the land in 1955," I countered.

"It might have been, but he visited the area several times before that. Here's another entry, dated July of 1949:

"'My belly is heavy as my time grows near. I think Tiger has finally accepted defeat. He announced at dinner that we will accept Ashton Montgomery's offer to provide fare for our travel east in exchange for the deed to our land. It breaks my heart to leave, but staying seems unwise. Most have already accepted Mr. Montgomery's offer, and the town is but a skeleton of what it once had been.'"

"Wow. The journal makes it sound like Ashton Montgomery practically stole the land where he built this town."

"Maybe. But maybe not. The gold had run dry. The town would have died anyway. Maybe Mr. Montgomery had selfish reasons for hurrying the death of Devil's Den, but it seems unlikely it would have survived no matter what."

"Are you sure you're only nine?" I asked.

Alex laughed. "Yeah. Why do you ask?"

"You just seem so very wise and insightful for a nine-year-old."

"I'm almost ten, and everyone tells me I have an old soul. Plus I have an IQ of 165 and I've been trained by my parents to think clearly and act appropriately ever since I was very young."

"Maybe. But you really are exceptional."

Alex hugged me. "Thanks. I really like you, too. Scooter told me he's going to be in your wedding. Do you think I could come?"

"I'd love for you to be here. Charlie and Bella are going to be the ring bearers; maybe you and Scooter can walk them down the aisle."

"Really?" Alex smiled. "I can be *in* the wedding?"

"I'd love nothing more."

I was nervous as I sat next to Zak and Levi that evening, waiting for the play to begin. Ellie hadn't arrived yet, but we'd saved her a seat. I'd never before experienced the anxiety parents must feel every time their adorable children took to the stage, exposing themselves for all the world to see. Neither Scooter nor Alex seemed particularly nervous, so I supposed this malady was limited to parents or parent surrogates.

My own mom and dad were sitting three rows back, next to Pappy, Hazel, and Phyllis. It seemed like most of the town had come out for this very special Christmas play. Carols played over the loudspeaker as we sat crowded together.

"I hope Alex remembers her lines," I whispered to Zak.

"Don't worry; she'll be fine. I heard her practicing earlier today and she totally had it down."

"I guess." I clung to Zak's hand. "I'd just hate to see her be embarrassed if she missed a cue or mixed up her dialogue."

Zak put his arm around me in a gesture of support.

"Sorry I'm late." Ellie slid into the chair next to me. "I had a last-minute call from Peter."

"How is lover boy?" Levi asked snidely.

"He's fine. But he needs a favor. From you, actually." Ellie turned toward me. "His grandmother is in the hospital and it isn't looking good."

"I'm sorry to hear that," I responded.

"He's leaving for the East Coast tomorrow. He was supposed to go to Alaska on Friday to deliver a dog he's been training for the search-and-rescue team in a little town called Moosehead. There's some urgency involved because the S and R dog they've been using was injured and had to be retired. He wanted to know if there was any way you could deliver Sitka in his place."

I looked at Zak. "How about it? The kids are leaving on Thursday."

Zak shrugged. "Fine by me. It might be fun to go to Alaska."

"I'm off until January 5," Levi chimed in. "I've never been to Alaska but have always wanted to go. I don't suppose there's room on the flight for an additional person?"

"I'll see if I can charter my friend's jet," Zak decided. "That way Zoe can bring Charlie, which I'm sure she'll want to do, and Sitka can fly first class rather than cargo."

"If we're all going I'll see if Kelly can cover for me at the Beach Hut," Ellie chimed in. "Peter was planning to stay with one of the guys, but I bet there's a house we can rent for the week."

"I'll look into it when we get home this evening," Zak promised.

A trip to Alaska sounded like just the type of adventure I needed to take my mind off the empty nest syndrome I was certain I was going to experience when the kids left.

"Either way I'll take Sitka," I confirmed.

"Great." Ellie hugged me. "I'm going to call Peter back right now. He'll be so relieved. He wanted someone who knew how to handle a valuable dog to take the trip with him."

The Christmas carols that had been playing in the background were turned off as the actors prepared to come onstage.

Levi frowned. "I guess I should figure out what to do with Karloff. I'm not used to having to worry about doggie care."

"Bring him to Zak's. I'll have Ellie drop off Shep as well, and I'll ask Tiffany to stay at the house. I'll need someone to look after Bella, Marlow, and Spade anyway."

"Great." Levi smiled. "I'm really looking forward to a change of scenery after all the stress of the past few months."

I nervously gripped Zak's hand as a loud crash could be heard from just behind the closed curtain. I hoped Scooter hadn't been responsible for the commotion. He'd behaved so much better than he had just a few months ago, but he still had the energy level of two little boys in one.

"Okay," Ellie whispered as she returned to her chair just as the lights were going down. "Peter is going to bring Sitka by your house tomorrow so he can go over all the special commands he's been taught. He said to call him in the morning to arrange a time. I'll text you his cell number. His flight doesn't leave until five. It was the earliest one he could get on Christmas Eve."

"Great," I whispered back as Alex, dressed in a red velvet dress with a large black bow in the back, wandered onto the stage in her brand-new black patent leather shoes.

"Doesn't she look beautiful?" I felt myself tear up as she walked to the center of the stage and began to recite her opening lines.

"She really does." Zak squeezed my hand.

As it turned out, the play was wonderful, and all the kids remembered their lines. Tawny had done a good job of matching the individual roles with each child's ability. After the play Tawny invited everyone to share punch and cookies in the lobby. There's something really satisfying about having other members of your community congratulate you on what a wonderful job your child's done, even if she isn't really your child.

"So is everything all set?" I asked Zak as we began to get ready for bed that evening.

"I spoke to Jake Carrington, the leader of the Moosehead Search and Rescue team, and he confirmed that there's a summer house we can stay in, and that someone will be at the airport on Friday to pick us up. I gave him an arrival estimate, but we can call him when we have an exact time."

"And the jet?"

"All set."

Zak began to sort through the pockets of the jeans I'd worn that day before changing for the play prior to tossing them in the washer. I have to admit I'm notorious for leaving things in my pockets that end up getting washed and dried. Rather than lecturing me on my oversight, as many boyfriends less cool than Zak would, he just takes it upon himself to do the sorting.

"What's this?" Zak held up the note I'd found in the cabin that morning.

I explained to him where I'd found it and what I thought it might be. To be honest, I'd forgotten all about it. "The numbers look like some sort of code, but I haven't had time to really delve into it."

"I think the numbers on the left might be dates," Zak said.

There were ten sets of four numbers, the first of which was 0519 and the last 1108. If you looked at the numbers closely they did appear to increase sequentially.

"Okay then, what about the second set of numbers?" I asked.

Zak looked at them for a few moments. "It's hard to say for certain, but I'm going to go out on a limb and say that they might be routing numbers followed by a dollar amount. Look at the first one: 1162408729-5500. If I had to guess I'd say that the first set of numbers is associated with a bank routing number and the last set is a dollar amount."

I frowned. "How do you know that?"

Zak laughed. "I have a lot of money. I make a lot of electronic deposits. I bet if we can find the bank the money was deposited into and the account number, we'll find ten deposits totaling over fifty grand banked on the dates corresponding to the numbers on the left."

"These must be the deposits Boomer made from the drug money he collected," I hypothesized.

"Maybe, but the guys on the team, with the exception of Jett, all came out clean. Who's Boomer selling the steroids to, if he is indeed dealing?"

"Good point," I had to admit. "What do you think that last number is?"

The last number on the sheet was much longer, with more dashes, and didn't fit the pattern of the others.

"I'm not sure. I'm going to go downstairs to my office to try a few things. If you're tired you can go on to bed."

"No. I'll come with you. Now you have me interested. It would be really great to get this all wrapped up before Christmas."

I made some hot cocoa while Zak did his thing. The house was dark except for the flicker of the battery-operated candles I'd set around the house and the flames from the fireplace. I clicked on the colored lights on the Christmas tree and the mantel. It was snowing outside and the house was warm and festive. I was having a hard time reconciling my feelings of contentment with the fact that we were up late investigating the brutal murder of a perfectly nice woman I'd grown to care about and admire over the past few weeks.

I turned off the kitchen light behind me as I carried two cups of chocolatey goodness into Zak's office. It was after midnight and I knew tomorrow was going to be a long day. A very long day, if the degree of excitement both kids had been exhibiting was any indication. I already had more things to do on my mental to-do list than was manageable. I really should let this whole murder investigation go. Salinger would track down the bad guy. Eventually. Maybe.

"I think I might have found something," Zak said as I set a hot beverage down next to him. "I took a chance that the deposits were made on the local bank, and it looks like they were."

"And?" I prompted.

"The deposits were made into Joe Lamé's account. The first deposit was made in May and the last one in November. And here's the interesting thing—"

"There's more?" I asked.

"A large chunk of the money was transferred out of the account a few weeks ago. I haven't been able to track down where it went yet."

"But who was putting the money into Lamé's account in the first place?" I asked.

"Tom Jarratt."

Chapter 12

Both kids were up by six a.m. on Christmas Eve in spite of the fact that they'd gotten to bed late the night before. Even Alex was running around acting very much like a nine-year-old. Zak made a big breakfast while I got ready to head into town to run a few last-minute errands. We had seven people coming for dinner that evening in addition to the four of us, so Zak planned to spend the day in the kitchen.

Zak had spoken to Salinger, who was going to follow up with both Joe Lamé and Tom Jarratt about the exchange of cash. While there was nothing illegal about one person giving money to another, the fact that the note was found inside the cabin that seemed to be linked to the murder had Salinger thinking it was worth taking the time for a friendly chat with the two men, even on Christmas Eve.

By the time I completed my Christmas shopping it was getting late. I really needed to get home to clean up before our guests arrived, but I had to stop by the cabin to pick up the carousel I'd bought for Alex. It was such a special gift that I'd had Levi hide it for me. The tree sale had ended the previous day, and he'd decided to set out all the trees that were left with a sign stating that they were free. Originally, he'd planned to be open until noon today, but there weren't that many trees left and he wanted to return to his own apartment for the holiday.

I decided to call Zak to let him know I was on my way. Poor guy; I'd only intended to be gone for a few hours and ended up being away the entire day.

"Just one more stop," I promised as soon as Zak answered the phone.

"Did you find everything you were looking for?" he asked.

"I did. I just need to pick up Alex's carousel. I stopped by Levi's to get the key and we got to chatting. I'm sorry; I totally lost track of the time."

"He's going to be at our house for dinner in just over an hour," Zak reminded me.

"I know," I said as I pulled into the now deserted tree lot. "There's some stuff going on with him and Ellie that isn't appropriate for mixed company. Given the fact that the four of us are going to be sharing a small house for a week, I wanted to be sure things were worked out between them. I'll fill you in later. . . . That's odd."

"What's odd?" Zak asked.

"It looks like Levi left a light on in the cabin. No matter; I'll turn it off when I leave."

"By the way," Zak added as I used my key to access the building, "I heard from Salinger. He spoke to Lamé, who I guess was receiving kickbacks from Tom Jarratt for giving Boomer a job after the steroid scandal. And the most interesting thing is that the large withdrawal from the account was because someone found out and was blackmailing Lamé. You'll never guess who."

"Chelsea," I said as I stood face-to-face with the girl, who was holding a gun on me. She knocked the phone from my hand, so I wasn't able to hear Zak's reply.

I know I should have been terrified, but for some reason the only emotion I felt was outrage. "You killed Mrs. Jolly," I accused.

"I had to." Chelsea's hand was shaking. I noticed that the paneling on the wall where I'd found the box and the note had been ripped away.

"Why did you *have to*?" I asked. Zak knew where I was. All I needed to do was keep Chelsea from shooting me before the cavalry arrived.

"I didn't want to." Chelsea was crying. "But everything turned out to be so complicated. First Tom Jarratt let Coach Denton use the cabin without warning."

"You were hiding the steroids in the cabin," I fished.

"It seemed like a good place. Boomer had a key and the cabin was empty. Neither of us could risk keeping them at home."

"*You* were selling the steroids?" I asked.

"Selling them? No. We wouldn't do that. We were giving them to Jett."

"Why?" I asked.

"We wanted him to make it onto a good college team. Or at least *I* wanted him to get onto a good team. Boomer just wanted to sleep with me and was willing to help me in exchange for a few favors in the bedroom."

I grimaced. Why would someone as beautiful and talented as Chelsea prostitute herself for a few steroids?

My confusion must have been evident on my face because she began talking again. "Do you have any idea how hard I've worked to make sure I'll end up achieving my dream of being a pro football player's wife?"

"I guess not," I admitted.

"I tried for months to get Jett to take the drugs Boomer got, but he wouldn't. We even broke up for a while over the whole thing, when it looked like he was going to be overshadowed by Tyson. I love Jett and can barely tolerate Tyson, but if he was going to be the only one to go pro . . ."

"You would marry a man you can barely tolerate if it meant you could be a football player's wife?" The concept was totally baffling to me.

"Absolutely. But then I got the idea to give Jett the drugs in his food, and I got Boomer to help me. Jett started to do better and I saw my dream coming true, and then my dad announced that he couldn't afford to send me to either of the colleges Jett was considering. Talk about a letdown. I know if I let Jett go off to college without me, he'll end up finding someone else."

"So you decided to find your own money?" I guessed.

"Boomer knew his dad was bribing Lamé to give him a job in spite of the fact that he knew about the steroids, so I got the idea to blackmail him. He was afraid of the scandal as well as losing his job. If Mrs.

Jolly hadn't happened along I would have had everything I needed to become the pro wife I want to be. I couldn't let the old lady mess it up."

"Happened along? What exactly did she see?"

"She saw Boomer and me in the cabin when she arrived to take her photos. Boomer has something going on with Tyson. I'm not sure what, but he's been a lot harder to handle lately. He told me that he wasn't going to give me any more drugs, so I needed to convince him."

"So you slept with him."

"I had to," Chelsea insisted. "Anyway, the old broad walked in on us and started going on and on about how I'm a student and Boomer is a coach. She threatened to tell Lamé, and I knew he'd be forced to fire Boomer, which probably meant the leverage I had to get more money in the future would dry up."

"So you hit her on the head with a hammer."

"I told you." Chelsea was sobbing. Her hand was shaking so badly that I was afraid the gun was going to go off whether she intended it to or not. "I had to kill her. I couldn't let her ruin everything after I had gone to so much trouble."

I noticed Chelsea's arm drop. It occurred to me that if I timed it right I might be able to knock the gun out of her hand.

"Okay, I guess I can see why you had to do what you did. Being a pro ball player's wife would be really awesome. The parties. The clothes. The VIP treatment."

"Exactly."

"What I don't get is why you set up Coach Denton. I thought you liked him."

Chelsea looked confused. "What? I didn't set up Coach Denton."

"You used his hammer to kill Mrs. Jolly, and his hat was found at the scene."

"I used the hammer because it was handy."

"Boomer knows you killed Mrs. Jolly?"

"He was here when it happened. She came in and started yelling and I picked up the hammer and hit her."

"You hit her in the cabin?" I clarified.

"Yes. Just about where you're standing now. Why? What difference does it make?"

"There wasn't any blood on the floor."

Chelsea started to sob harder. "She bent over to pick up Boomer's jacket to use as proof and I hit her. She fell onto our clothes. Boomer helped me carry her out. There was so much blood."

"So you left Coach Denton's hat where you dumped the body to divert suspicion from the two of you?"

"No. Boomer was wearing the hat. I guess it fell off."

"Boomer was wearing the hat while you were having sex?"

This just couldn't get any more disturbing.

Chelsea blushed. "I saw it on the table and couldn't resist. The coach is a babe and Boomer is such a pig. It helped to fantasize about Coach Denton while we were . . . well you know. You won't tell him, will you?"

I looked at the gun, which was now pointing at the floor.

"Tell him?" Was the girl nuts? She was going to go to prison for murder and she was worried about Levi finding out she had a crush on him?

"It would be so embarrassing if he found out."

Chelsea seemed to lose focus for a second and I decided to make my move. I lunged for the gun and it went off two seconds before Zak came crashing through the door.

"Are you okay?" Zak pulled me into his arms.

"I'm okay, but Chelsea needs a doctor."

"Salinger is right behind me."

Zak knelt down to check Chelsea's pulse. "She seems fine. I think the gunshot to her leg is just a scratch."

"I didn't mean to hurt her. I just wanted to get the gun so she couldn't shoot me."

"She's fine." Zak hugged me again. We could hear sirens in the distance. "I think she just passed out. It smells like she'd been drinking. A lot."

I let out a breath of relief just as Salinger came running in through the open door.

"At least Salinger didn't keep you until all hours of the night," Zak said to me a couple of hours later, as we sat at the kitchen table eating the leftovers from the meal he'd made and the others had enjoyed while Zak and I had given our statements.

"He was actually pretty decent about the whole thing. As soon as Dad and Levi finish the dishes we can get on with the rest of the Christmas Eve festivities."

"What did you have in mind?" Zak asked.

"When I was a little girl Pappy always read 'The Night Before Christmas,' and Dad always read the birth of Jesus from the Book of Luke. I've asked them both to do so tonight. I got stockings for the kids that I thought they could hang, and of course there's the traditional setting out of the milk and cookies."

"And the presents?" Zak asked.

"I thought I'd let them each open one tonight, and then they can open the rest in the morning. I still need to wrap the gifts I got today."

"It's a good thing I reserved the jet to take them to Scooter's grandparents. There's no way they'd fit all of the stuff you bought into their carry-ons."

"I'm really sort of sad they're leaving earlier than they originally were going to, but I am looking forward to visiting Alaska and delivering Sitka to his new home."

Peter had brought Sitka by earlier and he was in the living room with the guests and the other dogs.

"And I'm looking forward to us having some alone time." Zak kissed me on the side of the nose.

"Alone time? There'll be four of us in a pretty small house."

"Okay, so maybe when we get home from Alaska. Why don't you go join the others and I'll clean this up?"

"I can do it," I insisted.

"I know you *can* do it, but I'm going to do it; now scoot."

I kissed Zak on the lips and then did as directed. I stood in the entry, where the dining area merged with the living room. Levi was embattled in a video game with Scooter, while Mom sat on the sofa with Alex and Harper, looking at a picture book. Dad, Pappy, and Hazel were sitting around the card table, discussing the newest controversy in the town council, but Ellie was nowhere in sight. I pulled on my down jacket and headed out onto the deck that overlooked the lake. Zak had built a fire in the pit, but it was pretty cold, so everyone else was inside.

"It's freezing out here," I commented as I joined Ellie, who was sitting by the fire looking out at the lake.

"Maybe. But it's beautiful as well. And it's really not so bad with the fire."

"Any particular reason you're sitting out here by yourself?" I asked.

"Just thinking."

I brushed the snow off the bench next to Ellie and sat down. "Is there anything you want to talk about?"

Ellie sat quietly, looking off into the distance.

"Or not. Sitting in silence is good, too," I decided.

"I love Levi."

"I know."

"I want him in my life. And not just as a friend."

I decided to wait for her to continue.

"I want children so bad. I see how great Levi is with Scooter and I know what a fantastic dad he would be. It makes me sad that he can't see it as well. I know I should hold out for the children I want, but I can't picture not having Levi in my life. And if I'm totally honest, I have to admit that at some point this friends-but-more-than-friends thing is going to stop working."

I wound the fingers of my hand through Ellie's. I wanted to blurt out a solution, but the reality was that I didn't have one.

"I guess what I've decided to do is go with my heart and hope for the best. I know Levi says he doesn't want children, but six month ago he didn't want to be tied down with a pet and now he adores Karloff. I think I'm going to take a chance and commit to him and just hope that someday he'll be ready to take the next step."

"And if he never is?" I had to ask.

Ellie took a deep breath. "If he never is, then I guess I'll deal with it. I've thought about it a lot, and I'd rather be with Levi and never have children than have children with someone else."

I hugged Ellie and prayed her heart wouldn't be broken. I loved both her and Levi so much and just wanted them to be happy.

"Have you told him?" I asked.

"No," she said. "I guess I'm waiting for the right time."

I looked in through the window. Levi and Scooter were chest-butting each other, although Scooter was standing on the coffee table. Zak was laughing and Harper was clapping and screaming with delight.

"It's Christmas Eve," I reminded her. "A night of magic and new hope. I can't think of a better time for new beginnings."

"You think?"

I squeezed Ellie's hand. "Yeah. I think."

"Playing Santa is a lot of hard work." Zak yawned, much later that evening.

"Tell me about it. Do you think all of this will fit in the jet?"

"It's a big jet," Zak said, "but I'm not sure it will all fit in their dorm rooms. Maybe we should just dedicate the two rooms the kids are staying in to them, and then they can leave most of this stuff here for their next visit. I doubt they'll need snowboards or skateboards at school anyway."

I leaned my head on Zak's shoulder. "That's a good idea. Lord knows we have enough extra rooms. Do you think Alex's parents will let her come again?"

"I think they will," Zak answered. "I've spoken to her mother twice since she's been here. She was thrilled we took her in for the holiday. I know this is hard to believe, but I got the feeling that trying to accommodate her for school breaks was nothing more than a burden."

"The woman has no idea what she's missing."

"I made a comment along the lines that maybe she could come for a visit over the summer and her mom was practically begging me to pick her up at school and bring her back here when the school year was over. It seems she and Alex's father have some big project that will change the world, and it would be such a relief if Alex wasn't underfoot."

I turned and looked at Zak. "Can we?"

"Do you want to?"

"I do."

"Good, 'cause I do, too."

I leaned back into the sofa. "Look at us doing the parenting thing. And so well."

Zak ran a finger along my cheek and down my neck. "I guess we're pretty awesome at this parenting stuff."

"It's easier that they're already potty trained." I laughed.

Zak leaned in and kissed me. "I'm sure we'll master potty training when the time comes."

"Yeah." I deepened the kiss. "When the time comes." I ran my hands up Zak's back under his sweater.

"I figure we maybe have four hours until the kids will wake us up," Zak commented.

"I guess we should go to bed."

"Do you remember your Christmas wish?" Zak grinned.

"My Christmas wish?" I asked.

"Yeah." Zak nibbled on my neck. "The one you asked Santa Zak for the other day in the sleigh."

"Oh, that Christmas wish." I grinned back.

"We have four hours."

"Four hours is plenty enough time, and from where I'm sitting, sleeping is highly overrated."

Zak picked me up and carried me up the stairs. I wrapped my arms around his neck and rested my head against his chest. I could hear his heart beating against my ear, and somehow I knew we were destined to create a big, sloppy family. Maybe not tonight. Maybe not even next year. But who knew? Maybe this really was a magical night of new hope and new beginnings.

USA Today bestselling author, Kathi Daley, lives in beautiful Lake Tahoe with her husband, children, and grandchildren. When she isn't writing, she likes spending time hiking the miles of desolate trails surrounding her home. She has authored more than a hundred and fifty books in thirteen series set in twelve different states. Kathi enjoys traveling to the locations she writes about to generate inspiration and add authenticity to her descriptions. Find out more about her books at www.kathidaley.com

Made in United States
North Haven, CT
24 May 2025

69188121R00095